FATHER OF LIES

THE COMPLETE SERIES

STEVE STRED

BVP

Father of Lies: The Complete Series

Steve Stred

Covers by Mason McDonald

Formatting by Ross Jeffery

Edited by David Sodergren

Foreword by Sonora Taylor

Black Void Publishing

1st Edition 2021

Ebook ISBN - 978-1-990260-09-4

Paperback ISBN - 978-1-990260-10-0

Hardcover ISBN - 978-1-990260-11-7

Ritual – Black Void Publishing. Originally published October 1, 2019

Ebook ISBN - B07YBL2PF8

Paperback ISBN - 9781695441590

COMMUNION – Black Void Publishing. Originally published May 6, 2020

Ebook ISBN - B0879D3TS1

Paperback ISBN – 9781777157111

Sacrament – Black Void Publishing. Originally published June 1, 2021

Ebook ISBN - B094SK5ZPT

Paperback ISBN - B094SK5ZPT

I still think about the first visceral detail that Steve Stred scared me with. I read an advanced copy of his novella, "The Girl Who Hid in the Trees." In the opening prologue, an evil spirit in the woods rips out the spine of an unlucky person. But Stred doesn't simply say, "Their spine was ripped out." He detailed it in just the right amount so that to this day, I still shudder and clench my back muscles when I think about it.

I met Stred online around the time I released my second novel, Without Condition. We became fast friends, and started reading and reviewing each other's work (though Stred, who writes for Kendall Reviews as well as his personal blog, is much more gifted at reviewing than I am).

When Stred announced a new novella called "Ritual," I was intrigued by both the cover—a lone cross on a rainy and shadowy hill—and the premise. I said yes as soon as he asked me to read an advanced copy. I loaded it on my Kindle and started to read it on my bus ride into work.

I was immediately captivated by Brad, a man so entrenched with a mysterious cult that he couldn't see how horrifying his predicament was. Stred's prose brought me into Brad's mentality in a way that chilled me more than every awful thing happening to him and other members of the cult that were under the power of Father. Much like the ripped spine in "The Girl Who Hid in the Trees," I can still feel that sense of powerless dread when I remember the events of "Ritual." Stred wrote something special, a cult novella that showed the horrors of the cult, but more importantly, showed the devastating impact that cult had on one man's psyche.

"Ritual" is a powerhouse on its own, but when Stred announced a sequel, I was ecstatic. I couldn't wait to learn more about this unique world Stred built and to feel that dread once more. "Communion" did not disappoint, diving further into the depravity that Father and his daughter have in mind to summon the end of days itself. "Communion" moved beyond the individual impact on Brad and showed just how dangerous this cult was—even to non-believers. "Sacrament" expands on the reach of one cult's dogma with a monstrous end for any and all in the proximity of Father and his family.

Through the Father of Lies trilogy, Stred has created a cult series that shows its dangers via the people involved, as opposed to gross-out rituals or exploitative shock. The scariest moments in the trilogy come from the devotion of Father's followers. Stred's uncanny ability to make readers feel the horrors experienced are mastered in these stories, for the feelings go deeper than flesh and bone—they penetrate the mind.

FOREWORD

I hope you enjoy the Father of Lies trilogy as much as I did. Sit back, relax, and dive in—and maybe grab a blanket. You're guaranteed to shiver.
Sonora Taylor
2021

-A NOVELLA-
RITUAL
STEVE STRED

PART I

Psalm 102:9
For I have eaten ashes like bread,
and mingled my drink with weeping

All across the mountain, the man led his sheep.
All across the blackness, the devil watched him weep.
The time would come,
The flock would run,
As the horned beast, he did creep.

M onday mornings were always the hardest for Brad. The sun shone into his room, little particles of dust dancing through the light. He rubbed his eyes and yawned, wishing he was still sleeping. The weekends were normally busy, but with the deadline looming, he'd have to fit in more than normal over those two days. He stood and opened the door of his cheap closet to see what clean clothes he had. He owned three pairs of pants and five work shirts, which let him get through his work week without garnering stares or any snide comments. He grabbed one of the pairs of black slacks and a grey dress shirt and laid them over the back of his plastic outdoor patio chair that sat at the foot of his bed. He went to the washroom and looked into the mirror, thinking back over the weekend.

BRAD HAD WORKED HARD to create routine during the weekends. His week was based around routine so he ensured the weekend would be controlled as well. He wasn't a fan of surprises or chaos. He'd pick up the groceries he would need for the week, read his bible, mow the lawn (the blasted grass was growing so fast now, he had to cut it every weekend), and then read more of his bible. That was his normal Saturday.

Sundays brought a whole other mess of busy. Laundry, bible, vacuuming, worship, bible study, soup kitchen, nap, bible, and then America's Funniest Videos. He found while his routine was great, he still needed to relax a bit, wind down some and nothing was better than watching people on tape doing something funny. He'd find himself laughing so hard at his small tube TV that he'd be crying or get the hiccups. He used to enjoy watching stand-up comedy specials, but found lately the men were too vulgar and the women spent too much time discussing their feminine problems. He wasn't interested in their sinful ways, so he stopped watching those and focused on wholesome family programming.

Now, with the impending deadline (vigorously circled in red sharpie on his calendar) approaching, Brad was doing double time on the weekend in preparation. This explained why he was moving so slowly this Monday morning.

Last Friday after work, Brad had made the trip to the hardware store and replenished some supplies that were getting low. The group would be happy to see that Brad had completed this task on Friday. It would save them valuable time over the following days. Next Brad went to the art supply store and the candle store. The amount of candles they burned never ceased to amaze him. Finally he went to the dry cleaners and picked up the robes for the flock. He had to make three trips to his car, struggling under the weight of the thick garments.

Normally Brad tried to get to sleep early on Friday nights. His tasks took him until almost nine, so by the time he ate and read some passages, it was pushing midnight. *No worries*, he thought, *all in due time. I'll get the sleep I so deserve. I've done what's been asked of me.*

Saturday arrived like a boxer punching him after the bell. It took him a moment to get his bearings, sitting up in bed, sore and swollen. Although he'd never touched a drop of alcohol in his life, he imagined this was what a hangover would feel like. *Shouldn't have had all those fast food burgers so late*, he pondered. *Too much sodium. Not good, no sir-ee. Feet will be swollen and eyes with be puffy.*

The sun had just poked its shiny face into Brad's stark bare bedroom. He did his morning yoga routine, enjoying the feeling of stretching in the nude and felt the tight, scarred skin on his back unknot as he moved. He deserved every lashing he'd ever received, but the skin certainly wasn't too fond of the sensation.

After he had dressed, brushed his teeth and used the electric shaver to quickly get rid of the short stubble, he made some toast and read through a few verses while drinking some tea. Over the last few weeks he'd found his taste buds had left him. Now everything filled his mouth with the sensation of eating charcoal, as if each morsel of food had been marinated in a bed of coals. Once he made it through breakfast, it was time to start the day.

This Saturday featured more of the same. Repetition, repetition, repetition. Lawn mown, bible read, groceries obtained and more bible read. He also folded the robes he'd picked up, shined the shoes that matched each robe and sharpened the ends of each pair of antlers attached to the head dress. He marvelled at the different thicknesses between the elk antlers and the caribou antlers. The goat's horns weren't as silky smooth as the larger antlers. He found four sets of antlers from animals he couldn't place. He'd make a note to research them later, but the length and curvature had him baffled. Then he went to meet with Father, where he received five lashes. He had indulged in some urges during week, when he'd witnessed a young lady's skirt blow up in the wind. He needed to pay for what he'd done to himself. Father made sure to not strike him hard enough to draw blood, but the welts would sting for some time. *More damage to the scars*, Brad thought, as he dabbed the area with a hand towel.

"Go my boy, and thank you for your honesty. *He* appreciates your candor."

Brad went home and applied some ointment to his wounds, wincing as they stung. It was only mid-afternoon, so he spent a few hours reading his bible, cringing when a few pages pulled out. He knew he needed a new bible. This one had been read well over 5,000 times, but the sentimental attachment he felt to his current edition made it hard to let go. The leather that wrapped the exterior was so well worn where his fingertips nestled, it was as though the Lord himself had made the copy just for Brad.

Flipping through the pages, he found a few that still had blood splattered on the deckled edges and when he arrived at the Revelation of John he found entire pages stained a dark red, the words hard to make out. He softly caressed the hardened fluid with his hand, smile on his face, excitement on his breath.

He woke up on Sunday in bed, blood-stained bible still open. He didn't remember falling asleep but as he started his stretching routine, he felt thankful he'd completed all of his Saturday tasks. If not, he would be in for more lashes.

After stretching, teeth brushing, shaving, and his ash flavoured breakfast, Brad looked at the calendar with joy. One more week of work before the deadline arrived. Next Sunday was coming fast, the date noted, the preparations in place. Well, almost in place. He just needed to finish up today's tasks. When he was chosen as the anointed one, he was beside himself. First he was angry and frustrated - *WHY ME?!* Then he was elated and cried tears of joy - *ME? OF COURSE ME!* He just wished he had some family members left to talk to about this. *They'd be proud of me*, he thought, tears dribbling slowly down this cheeks.

As the month moved along and the deadline inched closer, Brad knew the flock had made the right choice. He was going to do everything he could to make it perfect. He wouldn't fail them.

So that Sunday, Brad hurried out of the house and began completing his remaining tasks. When he got home, he did his laundry for the week, did the vacuuming, and did some light dusting, before heading to the soup kitchen. At the kitchen, many of the needful who came for lunch daily smiled warmly at him, while some babbled incoherently. A few who were lucid and not drugged or drunk congratulated him on his honour and wished him well. "Thank you," he would reply, while ladling out their portions. He always made sure to stir the soup, not wanting any of the liquid to settle at the bottom. "If you let it settle," his father used to tell him, "They'll taste the difference."

When he was done serving the needy, he helped clean up and then pulled out his trusty book to read for an hour, filling his mind with the Lord's kind words. Then he went and found Father and they spent some time going over the plans. Nothing could be done out of order and everything had to be just right. Brad knew *He* would help, but at the end of the day *He* had no pressure. It was just Brad who'd be put on the spot. Father suggested they meet again each night after work this week, so that Brad would feel comfortable and confident. It would ensure smooth sailing on Sunday. Brad thought that was a fantastic idea, and as Father unzipped Brad's jeans, Brad picked up the swish and lashed himself across the back, only finishing once he was spent.

CHAPTER TWO

Heading home, he couldn't wipe the grin off his face knowing this would be the best week of his life. Soon he'd be held in the highest esteem possible. That night he read more passages from The Revelation of John, occasionally licking at the pages crusted with old blood. It'd been thirty five years since the last performance was attempted and Brad wanted to ensure this one was a success. He drifted off to sleep that night with dreams of the gates opening wide, letting him in. Behind him his Angels carried the long train of his robe, waving to all as he walked by.

THE WORK WEEK meant Brad fell back into his normal work day routine. He was wrestled from his sleep by the sound of his alarm going off. He rolled out of bed, stretched, and then proceeded to shower. The water and soap caused him to dance and wiggle, burning the raised lashes on his shoulders and upper back. *The sting is my Lord's forgiveness, washing*

away my sins, he thought through gritted teeth. Once done, he brushed his teeth and gargled with mouthwash. Being the week of the deadline, he didn't shave. His facial hair grew so quickly that six days was all that he'd need to grow it out. Then he made some toast and tea. Eating the charcoal flavoured toast, he flipped his worn bible back to the start and began to reread it once again.

At 7:45 am sharp, he got in his car and drove to the parking lot. Once parked he walked over to the train platform. At precisely 8:00 am the train arrived and he stepped on. Twenty minutes later he arrived at his stop, disembarked and walked the two blocks to his work place. Entering the office, he went down the hallway to the kitchen. He put his lunch bag in the fridge (same shelf every day) then went straight to his cubicle. His shared his cubicle space with one other worker, Larry, who was already sitting at his computer, headset on. Brad didn't like Larry. He was brash, vulgar and a womanizer. Larry would go on and on about the despicable acts he'd done to females and would describe in great details the acts he wanted to perform on the females they worked with.

Upon his arrival, Larry looked up and smiled. His face always made Brad squirm inside. Every single thing about Larry's face grossed him out.

"Hey there douche bag, which ways it hanging?" The greeting caused Larry to start laughing uncontrollably until he had to stop due to a coughing fit. Brad was happy he was done laughing. When Larry laughed his double chin jiggled, his large, voluptuous man-boobs wobbled and his protruding stomach heaved up and down. How any female felt the need to share a bed with Larry was beyond Brad.

"Good morning Larry," he softly replied, turning on his

computer. While the machine started up he put his own headset on and made sure the desk top was in order. Pen – check. Coffee – check. Mouse on mousepad – check. Mini-fan blowing – check.

"Hey boner, your special date's coming up soon, eh?" Larry said, pointing at Brad's calendar with the circled Sunday. "Losing your virginity? Is it with a human or an animal?" This was apparently funny as well and made Larry laugh again to the point of coughing. *Just choke to death already*, Brad wished, watching the man's face grow redder and redder. *Or have a heart attack.*

At nine sharp the system automatically turned on and a screenshot flashed of what they would be selling today. On Brad's screen he was looking at a picture of a 32" flat screen TV from a company he didn't recognize. It had minimal features but was listed for an overinflated price of $300, plus shipping. Larry made a snorting sound, which Brad took to mean that he was looking at something he figured he could sell.

"What you got over there? I got a kid's bike for $50. All those bored housewives who are begging for my salami are gonna wanna take a ride on this." Larry sounded very excited. He'd be able to sell a number of those, which would bring him closer to his monthly bonus. Normally Brad would be a bit annoyed at the product before him, but Sunday was coming soon and he wasn't too worried about the bonus.

"Over priced TV," he replied. He heard Larry guffaw at his product. Then the screen shifted and a new pop up was in front of his face. This displayed the numbers that he would need to begin cold calling, looking to find a sucker to buy this product, sight unseen.

Dialling the first number he felt the nerves of anticipation leave when the person on the other end picked up.

"Hello?"

"Hello. This is Brad calling from Best Products with a fantastic offer you just can't deny." His sales voice always creeped him out. He felt like a voyeuristic pervert selling these products. Peering into people's lives without their permission. Pressuring them to buy something they didn't need.

"Sorry, not interested." This was followed by the familiar click of the phone as it was hung up. Thirteen more cold calls later and Brad finally got a fish on the line. By this time Larry had already sold eight bikes.

"Hello, this is Brad calling with an amazing offer on a TV. I am with Best Products and this is a deal you just can't afford to refuse."

On the other end, Brad could almost hear the wheels turning, as the person processed what they'd heard. "Yes, I actually do need a TV. My basement TV just crapped out on me. Tell me more, please."

Brad didn't believe it. Someone was actually interested in this TV? He rapidly read the script to the individual, which didn't take long due to the lack of features. "How much is it?" There it was. The question that always sunk the sale.

"$300 plus shipping, sir," Brad replied, awaiting the familiar click.

"Well that sounds like a great deal then. Perfect timing. I think I may just pick up a second one for my garage work area. I'll take two please."

Brad stared at the computer screen in shocked silence. He was dumbfounded. *Two?* That had never happened one single time since he'd started working for Best Products.

Fifteen years now. Brad started there the day after he gradu-ated high school and hadn't missed a single shift. Brad snapped out of his stupor and quickly got the credit card info from the man and processed the payment and shipping, which was an extra $200 for the two TV's before saying goodbye. He hung up before the man could change his mind.

"Holy crap. You sold two of those crappy boxes to that guy? Way to go you taint licker. You didn't even offer to blow him!"

Brad smiled at Larry's ridiculous compliment. Today he wouldn't even wish sinful thoughts against him.

After work Brad took the train back to his car, then drove to see Father. They spent another few hours rehearsing before Brad grabbed a leather belt. Father then enjoyed him as Brad whacked the belt against his thighs. When Father was done, Brad limped to his car and drove home. He ate dinner with an ice pack on his reddened, swollen thighs and then spent the remainder of the evening alternating between reading some scripture and looking at the poster of Abaddon overtop of his bed.

All the while the circled date on the calendar loomed.

PART II

All across the landscape, the winds blew the trees.
On the floor of his bedroom, he stayed on his knees.
The day grew near,
The flock would cheer,
And he hoped that his god heard his pleas.

Tuesday was Brad's second most favourite day of the week. Friday was the hands down favourite because it meant time for the weekend, but Tuesday was close behind for one reason; the day started off with donuts and a staff meeting.

Brad stretched, showered, brushed his teeth, didn't shave, then ate breakfast and read the opening of Revelation of John again. Once he was done eating his toast, he ripped out a blood caked page and dipped it into his tea. Once the page was good and soaked, he folded it twice and put it in his mouth. He savoured the texture as it sat on his tongue and then he ate it in two bites. He then drove his car to the train stop, parked, took the train and walked to the office.

Brad put his lunch bag in the kitchen fridge, went to his computer, turned it on, before proceeding to the staff board-room. There he found almost everyone already mingling, some sitting and dining on a smorgasbord of donuts and coffee. The Tuesday morning staff meeting was something Best Products had implemented almost five years ago. Upper management decided that the best way to get the work week started wasn't to meet Monday morning, but rather Tuesday. They figured that first thing Monday morning, none of the staff wanted to look at their bosses. They could work their first shift of the week in silence and hassle-free. So on Tuesday morning, management would then highlight Monday performers and go over performance goals for the week, and how the company was progressing in their monthly targets. Brad had just sat down when he noticed his supervisor arrive. It was then he realized Larry wasn't there yet. As the meeting started, Larry came rushing in, trying his best to go unnoticed.

He slid into the seat beside Brad, which to his chagrin was still uninhabited, and started to chomp down on a sugar-glazed donut.

"Thanks for saving me a seat you scrote," Larry quietly said, spitting a sprinkling of sugar onto Brad. "I wasn't," Brad politely said back, which he followed with a cheeky grin.

Much to Brad's annoyance, the manager singled him out for selling the two overpriced TV's the previous day. This was met with a round of applause by the group and Brad felt his face flush. Larry kept elbowing Brad in the shoulder, trying to get him to stand up, but Brad was steadfast in his desire to sit.

As the meeting wound down, the managers wished everyone a great day of sales ahead, before Eric, Brad's supervisor, asked him to hang back.

"Oh, oh," Larry chided, "someone's getting a spanking." He then winked at Brad before leaving the room.

"Brad, come here please," Eric asked, motioning for him to come over. Brad left his seat and approached Eric, who was standing there with two members of upper management.

Brad tried to smile warmly while he stood waiting for them to finish talking. When they were done, Eric turned to Brad and started talking to him, while putting one hand on his shoulder. Brad looked at the hand, uncomfortable with the contact, but felt it'd be rude if he pushed it off.

"Brad, my man! We three are blown away with your performance yesterday. Why? Well, no one, and I mean no one, has ever sold a single TV, let alone two to one person. So as a thank you, we want to offer you Friday off, with pay. Sound good?"

Brad was taken aback. *How nice was this offer?*

"That's very generous, sir. But if it's ok with you, may I have next Monday off please?"

"Of course. Sounds like the weekend's going to a rager! Need a day to recover, eh?" Eric responded, teasing him much like Larry would.

Brad just nodded before leaving and heading to his cubicle. Time to sell more TV's.

After work, Brad took the train to his car and then drove to see Father. When Brad arrived he found Father in the basement helping some of the misguided flock repent.

"This is what *He* wants for you all. Repent," Father growled as the cat-o-nine tails whistled through the air before making contact. Screams and cries of horror echoed throughout the room. Brad licked his lips at the sight of all of the wounds opening and leaking. He had to wipe the drool from his mouth as Father kept the punishment going. When Father saw that Brad was watching from the entrance he clapped his hands, getting everyone's attention.

"Look you vermin, look. The chosen is among us. Kneel before him and crawl. Crawl to him and kiss his feet. For it will be him to lead us. And it will be him to choose who will gain entry when the gates open and *He* is ready."

. . .

THE NAKED SWARM of sinners dropped to the floor and crawled to Brad, their sweaty skin rubbing and grinding against each other. Brad felt a stirring against his pants. He wished he wasn't responded but couldn't help it. He watched as breasts drooped and dangled, the nipples rubbing and splitting open against the old wood floor. He watched the sagging testicles wobble back and forth, like the udders of an engorged cow. His eyes stared hard at the masses of flesh. He gulped deeply when they arrived and the women's long hair cascaded onto his feet. They were kissing his shoes, the moist skin rubbing against his pants as they moved around him. The temperature in the room had increased by a dozen degrees easily. As the flock moved in a circle, first to him, then away, his dress pants were pushed and pulled as they worshipped his feet. The material rubbed against his unwanted excitement and before he knew what was happening he felt a release. He made a muffled grunt and locked eyes with Father who stared back in horror and anger. How dare the chosen one give in to such earthly pleasures? Brad would be lucky to leave Father tonight.

FATHER WHISTLED LOUDLY INDICATING it was time for them to be done. Once the group moved away from him, Brad hastily retreated to the washroom, needing to clean himself up. He heard Father shouting orders for the gathered to dress and leave at once. He gave instructions for them to all return on Friday for one last rehearsal.

. . .

THEN SILENCE. Brad listened. *Had Father left?* The loud pounding on the washroom door startled Brad but also answered his question. Father was not happy and wanted to see him now.

"BRAD? You need to come out at once. We need to rehearse. Everything must be perfect on Sunday."

He didn't sound angry, Brad thought, so he opened the door and stepped out. The cat-o-nine tails caught Brad directly on his face, busting his nose wide open and ripping off part of his left ear. He screamed and cried, dropping to the ground. The blood began to drip from his face as soon as it was horizontal. *I need to go to a hospital,* he thought. But before he could stand to leave he felt Father's presence behind him.

"Brad," he spoke between his rhythmical movements. "You must remember all of these moments we shared. I have *always* been there for you. I made sure you were chosen. So while you may think I'm too *hard* and unjust with some of my punishment, just remember, I did it so that *you* would be successful." He then stood up, tucked himself back into his pants, and tossed a towel at Brad. "You'll need that for both ends. Now clean up, we need to rehearse."

CHAPTER SIX

That night sleep wouldn't come.

Sunday was so close but felt so far away. Soon Brad would show the gathered that he was worthy of the title. Worthy of being called the *chosen*. His face was throbbing and his ear hurt to touch but he didn't care. His poster smiled at him and before he drifted away, Brad smiled a crooked grin back.

WEDNESDAY MORNING'S routine had one variance to the normal routine. Brad took a moment to admire his full, thick beard that was coming in nicely. He also applied some ointment to the cat-o-nine tails marks across his face and applied a butterfly bandage to his mangled ear. He was growing frustrated with the bandage not wanting to stick and worried he'd be late for work, but finally got it to comply and was out the door on time.

Arriving at work the only one to comment was, unsurprisingly, Larry.

"Wow, you look like a prostitute that was rode hard and put back wet."

"I don't know what that means, Larry," Brad replied, annoyed with his cubicle co-worker. His reply stopped Larry's laughing in its tracks.

"Come on player, you know what I mean. Right? What happened to you though? For real."

Brad already had his excuse prepared. He'd figured it would come up at some point but was annoyed it was Larry he was sharing it with.

"I heard a noise last night outside my place. When I went to investigate a raccoon attacked me."

Larry burst out laughing, the coughing fit coming fast and hard.

"A raccoon?" He asked as he stopped jiggling and wiped tears from his eyes.

"Yeah a raccoon. It hurt like all heck."

Brad ignored Larry for the rest of the day. He was so busy thinking about Sunday that he didn't sell a single TV.

THAT NIGHT AFTER WORK, Brad was happy to see that Father was alone when he arrived. The basement was starting to be decorated for the event with seats set out and the pews arranged for easy viewing. A raised platform was in the middle, ensuring Brad's performance would be seen by all.

"Brad, hello. Come, let's get started, we may have a visitor later."

The two quietly changed into their designated robes, before making their way onto the platform. Brad went through the steps, making sure to enunciate, ensuring his voice carried across the room. As he spoke, Father took his place behind him and flipped up his robe. Brad hadn't expected Father to *actually* go through his part, but he tried to keep focused. Brad made sure to relax as Father moved. It was necessary for Brad to be able to speak each and every word perfectly, no matter what was happening around him. Brad noticed Father was becoming louder and rougher as he read and found himself struggling to remain composed and focused. Thankfully a noise at the door caused Father to halt. Brad stopped reciting from the book and looked over.

A figure lurked at the entrance.

"Sheol. Welcome! Come, meet the divine one, the chosen."

Father handed Brad a paddle without any instructions and then stepped before him on the platform, taking a few moments to straighten out his robe. Father motioned at him and Brad started to read again, before he heard the soft padding sounds of the mystery guest move behind him. Two noises indicated the guest had climbed the platform and was now positioned behind Brad. As this figure, known as Sheol, met the distance between Brad and itself, a wide grin spread across Father's face.

Brad found it hard to read and the words became stiff and forced. The mystery guest was rough and the amount of hair (*or fur?*) Brad felt against his backside scared him. Soon though a guttural noise indicated rehearsal was done.

Father led the large figure out of the room, talking in tongues he did not understand, while Brad stood up gingerly. He could feel fluid coating his inner leg as he straightened and needed to use two towels to clean himself before getting dressed.

Brad focused on telling himself that it was all worth it. In the eyes of the Almighty and in the minds of the congregation, it would all be worth it. When the doors opened and they all crossed over, all the hurt he felt now would be long forgotten.

HE CRIED himself to sleep that night, towel wadded up and placed between his legs. Blood continued to flow and he wasn't sure if he should seek medical attention.

When sleep did overtake him, his dreams were filled with flames and hot coals burning his feet. A presence was always near, a large figure shrouded in darkness.

Before he woke he heard the sounds of a million bulls barrelling down on him in a narrow cobbled street.

Thursday morning's alarm was a noise he wished didn't sound. Brad was sore which caused him to move slowly. He tried to stretch but he was in too much discomfort to attempt any of the positions. He lingered in the shower longer than normal, biting the inside of his cheek as the warm water stung. He found he couldn't bring himself to finish his toast or his tea. He didn't spend any time reading that morning and ended up late for the train.

When he finally arrived at work, Larry made sure to make a big song and dance out of it.

"Ohhhhh, lookie, lookie! Mr. Sells-two-TV's is late today! And since when can we grow out our facial hair? Look at this," he said as he reached out and yanked hard on Brad's beard. "HEY, CUT IT OUT," Brad replied loudly, unintentionally drawing more attention to his tardiness than he wanted.

Eric came over at the commotion, face expressing his displeasure.

"What's going on here? Brad, just because we're giving

you Monday off with pay, doesn't mean you can show up whenever you want."

"I know, I'm sorry. I missed my train."

"Are you... ok... Brad? Your ear looks horrible."

Brad didn't reply, just sat down gingerly at his computer and put his headset on. Larry sat staring at him. Brad knew Larry wanted to reach over and smack him, but with Eric still standing there he wouldn't.

"Ok. Well. Carry on," Eric said to no one in particular, before walking away.

Brad knew the day was going to be a long one. He just hoped Larry would leave him alone.

BRAD FIDGETED the entire drive to see Father after work. He was sore and every little bump the car hit caused him to wince in pain. The shocks were poor and his seat was worn out. He knew there was only two rehearsals left with Saturday set aside for final preparations for the performance. *Only two more rehearsals*, he thought, *I can do this. No, I must do this.*

Arriving, Brad parked. As he got out of the car he saw a police cruiser back out and drive away. *Wonder what they wanted?* he thought as he entered, hearing chanting from below. He went to the kitchen and retrieved a bottle of water before heading down.

Entering the room he saw Father standing on the raised pedestal alone.

"Welcome, Brad."

"Thank you, Father. I heard chanting?"

"Ah, yes. I was playing a recorded chant from our last performance. Sheol was very enticed by it."

Brad looked around but saw they were alone.

"I saw a police car leaving when I arrived. Is everything ok?"

Father appeared to either ignore his question or decided to not answer it. Instead he took a large drink of water from a pitcher on a small table. Brad saw how little beads of water were building up all along the outside of the glass surface. When Father put the pitcher back down the water was no longer a crystal clear fluid, but had a stained red streak within, as though a drop of blood had been added.

"Let us commence our rehearsal. You know Brad. Whenever we rehearse, the bond I feel between us is truly remarkable. *He* feels closer than ever."

Brad just nodded before opening the bible and getting onto all fours. As he started to read, Father came over and inspected Brad's beard. He began to stroke it, smiling as his hand moved up and down over his coarse facial hair.

Even with the new pain Brad felt, he slept soundly that night. Tomorrow was Friday and then the weekend was upon them. Soon he would be The Chosen One and the non-believers would see.

His dreams that night were filled with a large gate swinging open, the sweet sounds of harps being played and his skin slowly being burned from his body as hot lava and ash rained down from above.

CHAPTER EIGHT

The next morning Brad was able to return to his morning routine, even if his body ached and he had great difficulty sitting at his table to eat breakfast. Brad arrived at work on time, which he hoped would wipe the smug look off of Larry's mug. Larry made his usual immature remarks about Brad and threw in a few about his beard, which had now grown down to the middle of his chest. Brad ignored him and put his headset on. A long weekend was ahead for him and he decided that today he was going to sell those TV's as best he could.

His relentlessness paid off. By lunch break he had already sold five TV's. By the end of the day that total had increased to thirteen. When quitting time arrived he powered down the computer, placed the headset on its hanger mounted on the side of the monitor, and left without saying goodbye to Larry.

He smiled thinking he'd never have to see that asshole again.

PART III

Psalm 1:6
For the LORD knoweth the way of the righteous: but the way
of the ungodly shall perish.

All across the aeons the stars swirled bright.
All across the pentagram, the candles shone their light.
The humans were back,
His soul was black,
As he descended upon the masses that night.

1929

The preparations had been painstakingly thorough. *God how they'd been thorough.*

Now all they needed to do was wait and rehearse.

Five more days and the gates would open and the stars would welcome them for all of eternity. Nathaniel knew *He'd* come. This was the first time in a century that someone with the chosen blood had come to prominence and he wasn't about to mess it up. *Not me. Not this time,* he thought.

It had been a complete accident that it would be Nathaniel who'd ascend anyways.

The discovery had occurred only a month ago. It had been during a celebration of the solstice, a time for their Lord, the stars and the moon to align, bringing forth Sheol with all glory. Nathaniel had started the evening out dancing, robe on, hair tied back. The beat was rhythmic and the gathered stomped and circled around the blazing flames. Reaching skyward they all felt the glow of the gates, they all soaked up the cosmic layers of eternity.

As the sun fully set and the Moon peaked high above

them, Nathaniel found himself dancing in the nude, hair untied, the only piece of clothing to adorn him - his sandals.

Then *it* happened.

The music was pounding, the group was chanting, and as Nathaniel made another circle around the flames he noticed a figure step out from behind a tree. The being was immense both physically and spiritually. It was calling to Nathaniel and he found he couldn't move in any direction but to it. He flowed over, leaving the group behind, his feet never touching the ground.

Once he was out of the light cast forth by the fire, Nathaniel was able to see in greater detail just who or better yet *what* the figure was. He recognized Abaddon, the exterminator, immediately. The creature's likeness adorned many of the murals and paintings hung throughout the acreage. Nathaniel knew they wanted to open up Sheol, to enter into the afterlife, into the underworld and be rejoined with their family members. Abaddon would resurrect their dead, open the black heavens and their souls would stream down and join them for all of time. Even thinking about it Nathaniel felt a wave of euphoria wash over his naked body.

When the great horned beast spoke, wings spreading wide, his fleeting moment of joy was buried deep beneath the surface.

"I've come, it is your time. We must meld together. The time of ascension is upon us. The blood of necessity flows through one of you. Let us open the black heavens, let us corrupt each other and bring forth the tortured. You've been chosen."

The beast then reached out and with the end of one sharp claw, traced a line down Nathaniel, starting at his forehead and ending at his naval. A light trail of blood dribbled forth.

He became aware the group behind him had stopped dancing and were now crowded around, staring in disbelief at the *thing* before them.

Father stepped forward and hushed the murmurs that had begun. With his hands he motioned for everyone to quiet. Once they all were, he turned to address the beast.

"We were told we'd be contacted. But how, may I ask, can we be sure you're the *one* that we need to follow?"

In a blur of movement, the nightmare burst forth and decapitated Father. The crowd screamed and shouted in disbelief as the creature stood there holding their leaders head in one clawed hand and his body in its other. Then it roared and blew onto the bloody stumps and pushed them back together. It enclosed its membranous wings around Father's body and a light emanated from deep within. The group stepped back collectively, unsure as to what was happening. Then the beast opened its wings and Father was standing there as though nothing had happened.

The air was electric now, a crackle and hum reverberated around the area. Then Father smiled, his eyes blinked and he spoke.

"I... I saw the black heavens. I saw the gates swing open and I watched in awe as we walked through."

A cheer rose up and people rushed forward, hugging Father, wanting to feel for themselves that he was alive. Tears streamed down all of their faces and Father giddily groped and squeezed, the attention fulfilling a base desire.

Nathaniel watched as the hoofed creature disappeared into the shadows. Once gone from his sight, he felt his feet return to the dirt below. He turned to head back to his hut and in doing so a hush went over the group. They all quickly knelt down and bowed their heads as he passed. As he arrived at the door to his place he felt a hand on his shoulder. Looking, he found Father standing there, smiling.

"Nathaniel, my son. It appears that you've been anointed by the guardian itself. Tomorrow, arise, knowing you will lead us to the chosen land."

He entered the run down shack and walked to his bed. Once he was on the mattress he found he was vibrating by what he'd experienced. He drifted off to sleep with visions of beasts ripping apart the group's limbs as an inferno blazed behind them.

They stood and clapped and some even whistled as he entered the mess hall for breakfast, the next morning.

Nathaniel felt his face flush as he went to get his tray of food. They didn't stop clapping until he sat, then they joined him with breaking some bread.

The thin line that'd been marked upon him was still slowly bleeding.

With preparations underway, Father invited Nathaniel on an excursion. He was told to wear his hiking boots and bring some water.

Nathaniel had an idea where they were heading.

He met Father where the beast had stood, near the old, large tree. Father wore a flowing robe and carried a thick walking stick and looked energized to be spending this time with Nathaniel.

They walked in silence for the first half hour, Father leading the way. They had left the compound and headed up into the rolling hills. This time of day the fear of rattlesnakes and mountain lions was low, both hiding from the smoldering heat.

Nathaniel had never made the pilgrimage to Preacher's Rock before. High above them, at the top of the mountain, a stone had long ago been placed. It had subsequently been formed into the shape of a throne, and the legends based on its reasons for existing were varied.

Today, Nathaniel didn't care what the hushed whispers

suggested it was for. He was sure he was going to find out. After a prolonged silence, Father stopped and surveyed the valley before them. It hadn't felt like they'd climbed so high, but looking back Nathaniel was surprised to see just how far up they'd gone.

"Nathaniel. My boy. Do you truly believe within your heart that *you're* the chosen one?"

Nathaniel caught a subtle tone of anger in Father's voice and took a half step away from the edge of the path, feeling uneasy with where this talk and hike might go.

"I... I'm not sure. I was just dancing, feeling the stars caress my soul, Father, when I was beckoned."

Father nodded and turned, heading further up. Nathaniel hoped they'd arrive at the top soon. *What if I just leave?* He pushed the thought away and followed the old man. He was impressed with Father's stamina. He was close to eighty years old. Had his *experience* with the creature altered him somehow?

Then they arrived and Nathaniel found himself in awe of the experience of seeing Preacher's Rock for the first time. The stone before them was nearly twenty feet tall and Nathaniel suspected if he stood before it and stretched his hands out to his sides, it'd be wider than that. Sure enough the inside section had been chiselled or carved out to create a throne.

"The creature who visited us. It put this here. So it could look down upon us and watch us from its perch. It's done that for millennia, waiting for a way to re-open the black heavens, return to its kingdom. Sheol is both a place and a personification, Nathaniel. It'll chew you up and spit you out."

Father's eyes watched his face intently, looking for a sign

of weakness or something to suggest the creature had been incorrect. When he saw none, he stepped forward and gently caressed Nathaniel's cheek with the back of his hand.

Nathaniel wasn't going to be the one to mess any of this up. Not him, not this time.

"Sit then, Nathaniel. Sit upon the throne at Preacher's Rock. The chosen one will sit and feel their soul merge with the black heavens, much like my soul experienced the darkness beyond. If you are not the chosen, you will burst into flames and you will be gone before the pain reaches your nerves."

Nathaniel wasn't expecting any of this and now didn't believe he wanted to sit on the mythical rock. He wasn't here to see if he'd live or die.

Father motioned hurriedly for Nathaniel to get on with it. Feeling himself shake, Nathaniel stepped forward and tentatively sat down onto the stony surface.

From far below, the group members of Father's flock heard an agonized scream from Preacher's Rock. A ball of flame shot skyward and the members cried out and rushed back into their decrepit living quarters. Pieces of rock rained down on the deserted area around the fire pit.

Sometime later, Father's voice boomed from the middle of the encampment, asking for everyone to come out and join him.

Once he was confident everyone had gathered in the opening, he smiled warmly.

"First, let me apologize for the terror you may have experienced. Nathaniel was not the chosen one. As instructed by our visitor the other night, I took him up to Preacher's Rock and had him sit. His sins were exposed and before I could offer any sort of penance, the black heaven's took him by flame."

The crowd groaned and screeched, shocked and saddened at what'd happened to Nathaniel.

"Quiet. Quiet down, please. Look – I know you're scared. But I can attest to what the other side is and what awaits us. Now, the winged one will arrive as planned. Finish the preparations. Remember, only darkness above."

He strode confidently from the group, one hand on his walking stick, the other filled with rocks, leaving them all to gather themselves.

CHAPTER THIRTEEN

The day of ascension had arrived.

Father was bustling about, filled with a resurgence of energy.

The flock had finished the final preparations late last night. Once done, they danced and drank wine around the fire, swaying with the waves sent forth by the lunar light.

Now this morning they awoke, feet shackled and locked into wooden stocks. Their hands and heads were imprisoned, thick pillory devices trapping them, heavy iron padlocks securing their position. They struggled to scream, but their heads were adorned with scold's bridles; heavy iron muzzles with a piece fitted into their mouths. Their muffled cries were soon drowned out by Father's chanting, his volume growing in intensity.

One of the members tried to flop around, which brought Father's wrath. He walked over and kicked the man hard in the ribs.

"Shut up! Shut your filthy mouth. The time of ascension is here!"

He dropped to his knees and raised his hands high above him, smiling to the blue sky above. He returned to his chanting, growing more and more frenzied, and as if they'd choreographed it, as he reached the height of his vocal limits, a dark cloud appeared, rapidly covering the sun. As the day was plunged into darkness, the group heard a swishing noise and a sound reminiscent of a heavy horse walking.

Then the beast appeared.

It walked by Father without any acknowledgement and with surgical precision began to behead all of the imprisoned parishioners.

The rest of the members began to thrash and struggle, unable to see what was coming but sensing something horrible was about to happen. They made a frantic, feeble attempt at escape and continued up until the moment their head was removed from their body.

Father stayed on his knees, eyes glazed over. The only sound were his low sobs.

Once the beast had finished, it stacked the heads in a pile before the man.

"Burn it. Burn it and live forever, Father."

Father stood as the cloud dissolved in the sky and the light of the sun returned. As the beast walked away, Father scrambled after him.

"What about me? I thought I'd be heading to the black heavens?"

"Did you not take any of the remains from Preacher's Rock?"

"Yes, I believed I was supposed to."

As the creature faded from view, it replied; "Then know your acceptance into the gates will come"

Father was left alone then, surrounded by bloody blank faces, gore and hoof prints. He waited a heartbeat before walking away, wanting to burn the heads shortly.

PART IV

Revelation 22:13
*I am Alpha and Omega, the beginning and the end, the first
and the last.*

All across the colony the watchers drank their tea.
All throughout the village their prayers let them see.
The day arrived,
Their hopes revived,
For soon the winged beast would set free.

Brad arrived for the final rehearsal. He found the flock was already there and dressed. He found it overwhelming to see them gathered as a group. If he could just see their faces he'd feel better, but the bark and antler masks they wore obscured any features that would give away their identity.

"Brad, welcome. We are ready to begin. Please, go get changed."

Father was standing in his white robe, gold rope tied tight around his waist. He wore his ceremonial necklace made from rocks. He never let any other members touch it, let alone inspect it. Brad left the room and entered the bathroom. He kicked off his shoes and pulled off his shirt. He began to pull off his pants when he heard a noise from one of the stalls. He looked, but saw nothing. He returned to the task of taking off his pants when movement caught his eye in the mirror. Looking at the reflection of the stall, he saw what appeared to be two long, twisted horns protruding above.

Something was in the stall.

Still using the mirror, he looked at the floor and saw a hoof. It was a dark obsidian color but was criss-crossed with numerous gouges. Then he heard a low hum with a chant being sung over top.

"*Sheol, Sheol, Sheol, Sheol,*" over and over. Still looking into the mirror, a dark substance began to pour forth from under the door. It was frothy and bubbling, as though coming to a boil as it spread. Brad turned, drawing the courage to look at the stall. When he looked *at* it, not in the mirror, he no longer saw horns or the fluid. He took a step towards the stall when the door to the bathroom pushed open, Father standing in the opening.

"We are waiting. Why have you not changed yet?"

"I, uh, saw..." Brad looked at the stall and found the door open, no one or no*thing* inside. No sign of the twisted horns or the hoof. Floor devoid of fluid.

"Hurry up, please." Father then left him alone again.

Brad hastily finished changing into his robe. As he put his shoes back on he felt something shift in his mouth. He felt around with his tongue and when he realized just what he was touching and what was wiggling in his mouth he gagged and rushed to the sink, spitting. He recoiled in horror as he saw the porcelain splattered with blood. Within the blood Brad found thirteen of his teeth. In the mirror he now saw a version of himself that made him cringe. His thick beard was caked with a dark paste of blood. His mouth now resembled a dentist's worst nightmare – teeth missing and gums destroyed. His nerves were pouring forth pain. He tried to rinse his mouth but the water only made the sensation worse. *How would he speak?*

It didn't matter. He had to continue on, push forth.

He steeled himself and exited the bathroom, waiting at

the predetermined place, away from the group, out of sight. No one paid any attention to Brad's current state. Father led them through the opening of the ceremony, leading up to Brad entering the room. Brad walked in, taking his spot on the pedestal. He then began to read. As the words fell from his mouth from memory, Brad worked hard not to slur any of them due to the missing teeth. As he approached the crescendo of his performance he heard the gathered throng begin to hum and chant.

"*Sheol, Sheol, Sheol, Sheol,*" they chanted. As Brad dropped to his knees, he caught movement to his right, and looking over saw two twisted horns protruding into the room from near the stairs. Before Brad realized what he was doing he also whispered *Sheol.* The windows exploded, glass spraying the group. The wind billowed in, blowing the pews haphazardly around the room. The masked worshippers screamed and scattered as Father yelled for everyone to remain calm.

Brad looked back over for the horns but they'd disappeared. The wind died down and the pews were moved back to the original configuration. The air returned to normal. Father was not happy.

"Flock. We're done for the day. We will see you on Sunday. Brad, stay behind." His tone of voice let Brad know he was in trouble.

As soon as it was just them, Father walked over and grabbed him by the throat, pushing him down into a pew.

"Listen, you *disgusting* sinful traitor. On Sunday, you *do not* say that name at ANY point! If that word so much as leaves your mouth you will find out the true meaning of pain. I worked hard for you to be chosen. DO. NOT. FAIL. ME."

Father then pulled his robe up, pushing Brad's head

under, before letting the robe drop. He pumped faster and faster feeling the remainder of Brad's teeth catch on his delicate skin but enjoying the release as each of the remaining teeth popped from their home. If someone were to walk in at that moment, they'd believe Father to be alone.

Father grabbed the back of Brad's head through the robe and pushed his face hard against his groin as he shuddered. Releasing his head, Brad reappeared, gasping for air, snot spilling from his nose, vomit running down his chin. His beard was a mix of red, white and green fluid.

"You are the most disgusting human *He* has even chosen," Father said as he spit in Brad's face and proceeded to unleash a torrent of cat-o-nine tail strikes on Brad's back. Brad wasn't aware he had the device and was surprised by the attack. Even through the thick canvass robe Brad's back blew open and blood burst forth.

Once Father was done he returned upstairs, leaving Brad crying in the pew.

That night Brad slept with a bucket beside his bed and towels on his back. It hurt him whenever he had to suddenly roll over and throw up. The pain was severe enough he contemplated just puking, but he didn't want to sleep in vomit. He found a few final fragments of teeth in the bottom of the bucket, but he didn't care anymore. Tomorrow was Saturday. The final day of preparations. He was delighted. He wouldn't need teeth anymore. Eternity was coming. He'd no longer feel pain.

He smiled a toothless smile, staring into the crooked eyes of Abaddon in the shadows, before sleep took hold.

CHAPTER SIXTEEN

At precisely eight on Saturday morning, thirteen members of the flock knocked on his door, once each. Brad answered the door, already dressed in his robe. He bowed at each member, then followed them from his small cottage, down the path, leaving his car behind. As they walked the members sang hymns and stopped to bless the children lining the way. Brad waved and kissed the newborn babies as he went and as offered. The members of the commune not participating in the ceremony were in the large kitchen preparing the night's feast and the nourishment for tomorrow's big event.

They arrived at the holy grounds, crossing where they normally danced under the moon. They paused and looked at the mountain behind them, taking a moment to reflect on where Preacher's Rock formerly resided. Then they entered through the opening in the dirt. Once inside they passed through the church. Brad looked into the kitchen as they made their way down the hallway and saw the workers preparing everything. He waved and carried on. Soon they arrived at the back sanctuary and the two males beside him guided him to the far corner. There a table had been set up with his decorations and adornments laid out. The two males removed their masks and Brad was surprised to see Eric and Larry.

"My Lord," Larry said, no sign of his sophomoric humour. Larry then began to apply thick white make up on Brad's face. Eric meanwhile was painting Brad's nails. Once they were done, two ladies came forward and applied the facial markings that were required. They wouldn't let Brad see the reference picture they kept looking at, wanting to ensure the pattern was perfect.

"Brad, our Lord, you are now ready for tomorrow's ceremony. Please come, feast and we will entertain you." Brad then followed Larry and Eric as they walked to the theatre area, leaving the ladies behind. Brad was then sat on a large throne made of cushions. A crown of twisted horns was brought forth and placed on his head. Before him the curtains parted and he was delighted to see various plays acted out. He laughed and sang along as he was fed grapes and strawberries. He found the fruit easy to mash up with his still bleeding and painful gums. Every so often someone would dab his lower lip and chin, cleaning up the mess of fruit and blood.

As night approached, the plays stopped and a large bonfire was lit outside. Brad joined the crowd and they sang and swayed as the moon danced with them. High above them, Preacher's Rock sat empty.

Tomorrow was Sunday and Brad had never been so excited.

As the sun arrived Sunday morning, the ceremony proceedings began. Brad was brought out of his slumber by the feeling of thirteen other members of the flock massaging his nude body with oil. He thanked each one with a kiss on the lips, then was helped out of his royal bed. His old mattress had been comfortable, but this bed was fit for a king. He put on his robe, had his face paint touched up and then the antler crown was placed on his head once again.

He walked through the gathered crowd and was surprised at the response; many cheered, but some were already bawling their eyes out, finally seeing *their* chosen one in the flesh. The procession arrived at the holy grounds and they entered through the opening in the dirt. They walked down the hallway to the entrance to the underground. They travelled down the steps before arriving at the raised pedestal. Already the pews were filled with the members of the congregation. They were in their robes, masks on. Father stood in the center of the pedestal and when he spotted Brad he spread his arms wide and smiled warmly.

"Come. Come my Son. Let us begin the festivities."

The gathered folks cheered and clapped, excited to be witness to history. Where the last performance had failed, this time the chosen one would ensure success.

Brad walked forward and as rehearsed, kneeled before Father.

"Brad. You've been chosen. The first one of our flock since 1929. Other congregations near us have professed to have had a member chosen, but all were ultimately frauds. Now, *He* is awaiting your earthly sacrifice to lead our group to safe passage. What say you before the naming takes place?"

Brad cleared his throat and looked around at the masks staring back at him expressionless.

"Let the ceremony begin. I *am* the chosen. *He* is waiting for me, for us. I will bring us together where we will live for eternity. To open the entrance to the black heavens, we must first feel the wrath for our earthly sins. Proceed."

As Brad spoke the word *proceed,* a chime sounded.

Outside the five hundred members of the commune had congregated in the courtyard. Everything was prepared, and the Chosen One was fit to proceed. They'd made their way first thing after Brad had passed, moving single file and had a ladle of liquid poured into a small clear plastic cup. As the chime sounded, every man, woman and child raised the small glass to toast their journey to come. Looking to the sky they brought the cup to their lips and drank their nourishment.

A casual bystander would be hard-pressed to see any reaction to the ingestion of the fluid, but up close things were already in motion. The small veins in the member's faces were beginning to expand and become visible, while their skin broke out in hives covered with a thick sheen of sweat.

Every muscle in their bodies began to shake and tremble, losing their abilities to have any fine motor-control. As if choreographed, every single clear cup dropped to the ground simultaneously. The hives now burst forth, pus and thick chunks of calcified capillaries pushing forth out of the new orifices. Blood bubbled and frothed from their ears and nostrils and soon the whites of their eyes also grew dark red before turning black. Each member was being boiled alive from the inside. The viscous gel burst from their eyes, causing a noise similar to the snapping of fingers to ring out as one thousand eyeballs popped at the same time.

From their mouths spurted thick foam, their lips cracked and turning to a curdled cheese. It was at this time the muscles in the legs failed and all five hundred members dropped to the ground, dead. A sizzling noise continued for some time as the internal temperature remained elevated and cooked the deceased from within. A hazy smoke arose from the bodies, the smell reminiscent of singed hair and over-cooked deli-meat.

Back inside, Father stepped forward, now standing directly in front of Brad. He slid a mask over Brad's face, made also of bark and antlers. Brad's mask possessed the beak of an eagle. He then placed a hand on each of his shoulders and spoke.

"You kneeled before Father as Brad. You rise before Father as the chosen one. As Belial!"

As the name of the ancient one echoed from the walls all of the candles erupted, flames burning brighter and higher. Brad stood now, his face burning. He focused on staying calm, feeling the mask liquefy and become one with his face.

"Thank you, Father. I will now recite the words. Within these words *We* will find *He*. The entrance between our earthly bodies and our immortal souls will open and accept us. Black heavens become our home."

As Brad spoke the air grew cold and the beast with twisted horns appeared from the dark near the stars. Brad knew this was no illusion. The beast moved forward as Brad continued, now speaking in a language he was never taught, nor heard before. As the words ended, he fell to his knees and raised his hands before him. The creature set a knife in his palms, leaned forward and kissed Brad, breathing into his mouth deeply. It then turned and walked back into the shadows.

Brad gripped the knife he'd received and felt its weight in his hands.

"Now. My children. Arise."

The congregation stood up from the pews, their attention hanging on every word Belial spoke.

"Disrobe."

The members removed their robes and stood naked except for their masks.

"We begin with the males."

The females in the pews then turned to the males beside each of them. They knelt down and retrieved the knives placed previously on the pews. Using a smooth, fluid motion, they cut off their sex organs. The men howled in pain, and as the blood flowed the flames of the candles burst forth again.

"Now. We finish the males."

The females then rose up and faced the man before them. In a quick slashing motion, they pulled the knife across the man's neck, causing a torrent of blood to fly forth. The men gurgled and spurted and dropped, their weight banging hard onto the pews before them.

"Now. We finish the females."

The women then turned to face Belial and Father. As they did, they looked above them and slashed their own necks. Choking and gagging, they fell upon the bodies of the dead men.

"I Belial, the worthless, the wicked, the opposition of David, call you forth Abaddon, call you forth Sheol, to rise. I *am* the chosen. *He* has beckoned me. I will take my place for eternity amongst you."

From the darkness a low growling began. The figure approached, hoofed and carrying its twisted horns above a disfigured face. It approached Father, who reached out and embraced it in a hug. He then disrobed and knelt before it on all fours. The beast mounted the man roughly and as it thrust Father turned bright red before the two burst into flames. As Father screamed and burned the beast grunted and groaned. Belial watched as Father's stone necklace scattered across the floor.

Belial became aware of a second guttural growling from behind him. Turning he spotted Abaddon. His visions made flesh. The demon's wings opened and closed, flexing in the confined space. The small nubs of horns on its head scraped along the ceiling as it approached, tongue out and hands grasping. Belial flipped up his robe and assumed the position. Fathers charred remains slowly turned into ash on the ground.

Abaddon quickly met Belial's backside and grabbed onto the antlers attached to his head. As he began to thrust, Belial spoke again in a language he didn't understand. Brad was still within this transformed body, but his voice was silenced below. The flames from the candles now reached the ceiling, catching the wood above on fire, starting to burn the room, the temperature soaring. Belial knew his timing had to be precise. As Abaddon increased in speed behind him, he grabbed the knife and held it before his neck. As Abaddon slammed into him, he knew the time was now.

"THE RITUAL IS NOW COMPLETE," he shouted as he slit his own throat - jugular pulsing blood in thick streams before him. Belial felt the beast behind him wrap its wings around them both. As he gagged and choked, the two of them burst into flames. He felt Abaddon caressing the mask on his face and licking his antlers. Then darkness, the black heavens having accepted them all.

Nobody noticed on Monday when Brad, Eric and Larry didn't show up for work. It wasn't until the end of the week that someone reported Eric as missing. The police went to his listed address for a wellness check but discovered the place was completely empty. They found the same thing when they did a wellness check on Larry. When they decided to check up on Brad, they drove the same route Brad drove every day until he was chosen.

Arriving at the fortified gate to the commune the police suspected something wasn't right. The first responder recognized what they were looking at immediately and placed the call to Detective Kramer.

etective Kramer had been kneeling down to inspect
the scene before him for so long that it pained him to
stand up, doing so when the second homicide detective
arrived.

When Kramer had arrived he had found a gathering of
onlookers already. He'd scanned the surrounding crowd,
sunglasses blurring out the blue and red lights. He was
looking for someone acting *off*. Someone out of place.
Nothing set off his Spidey sense, though. He figured the
lookie-loos were all there to see what a mass suicide looked
like. *Five hundred bodies outside. Why me?* He thought.

Now standing down in the basement of this place of
worship, he was creeped out and just wanted to leave.

"Jesus Christ. I was just here doing my normal check on
this crew. They always just smiled and said all was well.
Creepy, blank faces."

"Rough night?" He was asked as he groaned and cracked.

"Old age. What took so long, McKay?"

"Didn't ya hear? This ain't the only scene."

"How many?" He responded looking back at the chaos before him.

"Four verified, one pending. But based on what I've heard over the horn, I'd say it'll be five confirmed by days end."

"It's started again." He patted an officer standing nearby on the shoulder, then ducked under the crime scene tape.

Kramer walked back outside to his car, McKay close behind. He was certain he was gonna get sick. Thirty four years on the job, one year from retirement, and this gets tossed in his lap. He wouldn't be surprised if he looked at the cold case files and found it had been exactly ninety years to the day since the last event.

"Same layout? Same number of victims?"

He spoke quietly. He knew what the answer would be but he didn't want to hear McKay's response. He also knew that a number of reporters were loitering around, looking for any angle to run with. One wrong sound bite out of his mouth and goodbye pension.

"Yup. Five burned bodies, five pedestals. Not counting the numerous dead from ingestion of poison. And forensics has already confirmed the first three scenes were all done with a similar style weapon."

Kramer let out a pained exhalation. He knew that at each scene it would look random, but it was far from. The five pedestals would form a perfect star. And, more unsettling, when you plotted the GPS co-ordinates of each scene, another perfect pentagram would be revealed.

"It's returned."

McKay felt a ripple of fear pass over him at the tone in his partner's voice. He'd worked with Kramer for fifteen years now and had never seen the man flustered or scared. That was until now.

"I didn't think this would ever happen again. Not on my watch."

"What do you mean it's...?"

McKay tried to speak but was too late, Kramer had already driven away. He felt a shiver go through him, as though he was being watched by someone, but when he looked at the people milling around he didn't spot anyone out of the ordinary. He scanned the area but the only thing he spotted were dead bodies everywhere. He took one last look at the tall hill behind the property before heading back inside, noting just how cold the space was down below.

Looking at the bodies before him, he questioned just what Kramer was alluding too. His partner knew something, but wasn't willing to share. Did he know who this killer was that had cut off all of the men's privates and slit the throats of every man and woman? Not to mention the burned victims? He knelt down in the same spot Kramer had and looked at the nearest victim. Kramer seemed spooked by the facts presented to him. *He knew who did this, didn't he?*

Taking his time, he walked from victim to victim, ensuring he didn't interfere with any of the bodies. At each one he spent a few moments looking over the details before him. What was he missing? The first body, a woman, had received a single slash, for want of a better word. Straight across the throat. The angle suggested it was self-inflicted, but he wasn't a forensics expert. The next body was a male and was mutilated the same as the other males. Penis cut off, neck slit. *What the hell happened here?* McKay turned his attention from the bodies to the room. The glass looked to have exploded inwards and the roof had scorch marks on it. *Too bad they didn't have any cameras in here,* he thought.

Looking at the area around the pedestal he noticed some

bark and charred antlers. Stones lay around the burned body. *Must have been some weird Earth worshipping mask,* he pondered.

He decided he couldn't offer anything more here. He'd go find Kramer and wait for the various reports to come in. He'd probably need to do some groundwork for Kramer with the press, but that was just part of the job. *Maybe I'll try and get some time with some cold case files,* he thought as he made his way up the steps. As he walked to his car he spotted something glinting near the large fire pit in the middle of the yard. Walking over, he bent down and froze.

It was a piece of vertebrae. It had been removed so neatly that the mushy spinal column was still inside.

He took two quick steps over to some bushes and retched up his morning coffee.

Returning to look at the bone, he noticed something else.

In the dirt there were two hoof prints. The size was unnerving. He put one of his polished dress shoes beside it; size 13, and saw that the print was a good six inches longer. He saw a small trail leading away. He followed it for about twenty feet before they abruptly disappeared, as though whatever had made them had simply vanished.

His entire body went cold thinking about what may have killed all these people. A part of him hoped he'd never find out.

END

RITUAL

All across the mountain, the man led his sheep.
    All across the blackness, the devil watched him weep.
    The time would come,
    The flock would run,
    As the horned beast, he did creep.

All across the landscape, the winds blew the trees.
    On the floor of his bedroom, he stayed on his knees.
    The day grew near,
    The flock would cheer,
    And he hoped that his god heard his pleas.

All across the aeons the stars swirled bright.
    All across the pentagram, the candles shone their light.
    The humans were back,
    His soul was black,
    As he descended upon the masses that night.

All across the colony the watchers drank their tea.
    All throughout the village their prayers let them see.
    The day arrived,
    Their hopes revived,
    For soon the winged beast would set free.

ACKNOWLEDGMENTS

Thanks to everyone who took this for a ride before the release! All of those pre-release reviews have been great to see!

Thanks to all my friends and writing pals who keep helping and supporting.

Thanks to my family, for always believing I can get stuff accomplished.

Lastly, thanks to the readers. It's so cool that someone other than me reads my stuff!

Steve.

COMMUNION
STEVE STRED

For DIE!mond. Thank you for your support!

Job 1:7
The Lord said to Satan, "Where have you come from?"
Satan answered the Lord, "From roaming throughout the
earth, going back and forth on it."

CHAPTER ONE

Detective Marvin McKay sat at his desk looking at the shit show of reports and photos splayed out in disarray.

It had been a week since the discovery of the aftermath at the commune. Four other groups had committed mass suicides at the same time, but those turned out to be unrelated. For that he was thankful. It meant he wouldn't have to meet with other detectives, wouldn't have to read through hundreds of group emails every day.

But Jesus fucking Christ was he struggling with what he'd seen.

His partner, Kramer, had up and drove home from the scene of the crime, wrapped a length of rope around his neck, and stepped off the landing of his two-story house. A year from retirement, and he chose to leave without even a cake.

"What the fuck!" He yelled out, startling the officers who were still mulling around the precinct at three in the morning.

Wiping the spit from his lips, McKay shook his head and decided now was as good a time as any to refill his coffee.

Leaving his office, he saw a few eyes dart his way, but the officers knew to keep their distance.

Had he slept since learning Kramer hung himself? He didn't think so. He didn't care, he just wanted to figure out what the fuck had happened, and how to prevent this from turning into a full-blown copy-cat situation.

Reports from around the country had trickled across their desks. In Florida, a group of twenty-five males had chanted the name 'Sheol' over and over before opening fire on a church. Police had arrived and through returned gunfire, killed all of the men. The only thing that McKay found intriguing was that the men were nude from the neck down, their penises cut off, and they'd been wearing wooden masks. Similar to what they found near the altar in the basement of that pseudo temple.

McKay believed it was copycat bullshit. Unfortunately, video from the complex had already hit the internet.

Grabbing a cheap, shitty Styrofoam cup, he grabbed the carafe and poured some lukewarm coffee in, then followed that with four tablespoons of sugar, just enough to make it not taste like sewage.

As he walked back to his office, McKay caught the shape of someone standing near the intake desk. Stopping, he leaned back to get a better view.

Admiring the ass displayed in the tight dress, he changed course and made his way to the front desk.

"Officer Douglas, you need a hand here with this lady?" McKay asked, trying to sound chipper.

"Thanks, McKay. She says she has some info about," Douglas looked at his notepad, "someone named Brad? Said it has to do with the Kool-Aid cult." McKay tapped his shoulder, not wanting him to use that name in front of the public.

They hadn't found any writings or documents containing anything to officially name them or label them. The media had given them a few different monikers, but for now, McKay was fine to just refer to them as a file number.

"Well, I'm the detective in charge. Let's find an open interrogation room and we can sit and talk. Unless you'd prefer my office?"

"The interrogation room would be just fine," she replied.

McKay couldn't stop staring into her eyes. He'd never seen a color so radiant. Almost yellow. He presumed contacts, everyone was wearing some sort of jewelry now.

"Just wait here. I'll go get my notepad. Douglas, grab her a coffee or something while she waits, yeah?"

McKay shuffled off, smiling at his luck. Sometimes people were so desperate, worried they'd say something and end up in jail, they'd do just about *anything* to stay out of prison.

Anything.

Entering his office, McKay slipped off his belt and hung it over his chair.

Walking back to find the woman, he was counting on her being up for whatever, tonight.

Lord knew, he needed some relief.

"Miss... I'm sorry, I didn't catch your name," McKay said, looking at the notepad Douglas had handed him.

Taking a seat across from McKay, she looked even more radiant surrounded by the darkened background.

"I didn't give it. I want to make sure I'll be protected," she replied.

"Absolutely. That's what we do."

"You didn't protect Brad. Or the other followers. Has there been any sign of Father?"

McKay stared at her for some time, rolling around his head all the connections he'd made through background checks and interviews over the week. It felt like years since Kramer discovered the aftermath already.

"Look, it's a situation that's evolving, and I'm dealing with many working parts. So, let's just cut to the chase. What do you know? How are you connected? I don't need a name if you are worried about your safety."

She gave a nod, took a sip of her coffee, then examined the room.

"It's just us here. Three am. No cameras. I'm not recording this."

That seemed to soften her, her shoulders relaxing a bit.

"My name is unimportant. I knew Brad because he was the Chosen One. I knew Father, as he was *my* father. Detective McKay, I was a member of that cult. For my entire life, I lived and breathed our mantra of opening the black heavens. Of ascendency and immortality amongst the cosmos. Of living both *here* and *there*."

McKay watched her face, not seeing any ticks or quirks. If she was lying she was doing a damn fine job of it.

"That's great and all, but why come to me? Why now?"

Now it was her turn to run some scenarios through her mind. This made McKay uneasy. He was the one who was supposed to be in control. In this room, right now, he didn't feel like he was leading.

"I know you don't believe what I've said. I can assure you, I'm telling the truth. You don't understand everything you're dealing with. You don't understand what's to come here."

She sounded like she was on the brink of a panic attack. She had suddenly grown agitated, and McKay could swear she was starting to sweat.

"OK. Let's take a breather. Are you alright? Do you need something to eat? Refill on the coffee?"

She shook her head, her breathing settling dramatically.

McKay wished she was still amped up, he enjoyed watching her ample chest push up and down, straining against that thin material.

God, what I'd do to this slut, he thought.

He didn't have time to finish his thought, as a nail

slammed through the back of his palm, easily slicing through and penetrating the table below. He screamed in agony, looking at the woman before him.

Her eyes were wide, her teeth bared.

"I'm not going to fuck you, you piece of shit," she roared as she reared back and punched him square in the nose. His face burst open, blood and cartilage flying.

"Your blood plays a role that *he* needs played," she said, as she pushed the nail further into the table.

"Help!" He yelled, trying to pry his hand free from the table, the rusted nail holding firm.

"Preacher's Rock holds the secret. Go there. Study what I've left in your office. Just know, it's watching how this unfolds. Soon it'll unfold before you."

CHAPTER THREE

"What took so fucking long?"

McKay was furious at the slow response.

Between his hand and his nose, a lot of blood had collected on his lap and the table in the interrogation room.

The mysterious lady had disappeared and left him yelling for help for what felt like hours, his voice becoming hoarse and his throat feeling like sandpaper.

Officer Douglas had casually walked in, drinking some coffee. When he saw the extent of McKay's situation, he immediately called for a medic and then peppered McKay with questions.

Once the medic had bandaged the hand - Douglas informed McKay that the woman had vanished, but that she had in fact left a package on his desk.

"It's wrapped in butcher's paper," he'd said, nonchalantly.

"Is it fucking leaking anything?"

"Not sure."

"Not. Sure? What the actually fuck, Douglas? That bitch

just broke my nose and used a four-inch nail to fuse me to the fucking table. She left something in butcher's paper and you what? Didn't even investigate it? Fuck me, expect a reduction in duties real quick. Better call your union rep, motherfucker. When I get back from the ER, I'm filing papers."

Douglas stood stunned as McKay was led to the waiting ambulance by the medic.

CHAPTER FOUR

F our hours later, McKay returned to the precinct, elated to not walk in and see Douglas sitting at the intake desk.

He ignored the stares as he made his way to his office, dismayed to see that Douglas had been right – there on his desk was a wrapped package.

The brown butcher's paper sat like a square of radioactive material.

"You gonna open it?"

The voice from behind scared the shit of him, causing him to jump.

"Sorry, boss. Didn't mean to sneak up on you."

McKay looked, seeing Erickson standing there.

"All good, Erickson. I assume that loudmouth Douglas filled you in about last night's festivities?"

A quick nod answered.

McKay went and sat at his desk, staring at the package. He looked at the wrapping, the string around it and at the shape.

"You want me to call forensics? Get it dusted for prints?"

"Nah, I suspect it'll be a waste of time. I mean, fuck. How many prints did we get at that compound? Not one of them were in the system. This chick ain't going to be either."

"You sure boss? Freddie watched the tape from when she entered and he's pretty sure he hauled her in for assault a few months back."

This piqued his interest.

"Give Freddie a call, tell him we need to talk."

Erickson left, leaving the man alone with his delivery.

"Just what the fuck is in here?"

Finally, McKay worked up the nerve and grabbed one end of the bow. Pulling the string, it un-looped and fell away. Some of the brown paper popped up a bit, but McKay would have to pull it back to open it all the way.

Looking out into the work area, he could see a few officers at their desks leaning and lurching, trying to get a view.

"Whoever's interested in seeing what's in this, get over here!" He hollered out.

A bustle of activity from beyond the closed blinds of his office window led him to get up and turn the thin plastic twister to open them. The entire police force was standing on the other side.

This made him feel more confident, if not a bit worried that if a bomb was inside, the entire contingent of Precinct 32 would be eradicated with one detonation.

"Show time," he said, pulling the four corners of the paper back.

What the paper had been concealing was a very old looking box.

The gathered officers collectively leaned forward, craning to see what was on the box.

McKay looked at the lid, seeing carvings and lettering.

"What's it say?" someone called out.

McKay looked at the faces gathered around, feeling as though the room had suddenly increased in temperature.

"There's lettering carved into the top. Appears to be a stone box. It says *Nam hoc novum mundum venisti*. Is that Latin? Someone get me a translation," he asked, snapping his fingers.

"Yeah, Latin. Google Translate is showing that it means *'For a new world would come.'*"

McKay felt like his stomach contents were fighting to leave his body.

"What's carved on there?"

McKay looked at the officer who asked, wishing he'd not invited everyone to gather around.

"There is some sort of creature here. Long horns, goat-like face. The feet are hooves. Looks like the body is human," he said to the room.

"Satan?"

The noise of people murmuring agreement arose.

"I don't believe so," McKay replied. "If this has to do with what happened at the compound, nothing that we've found has been related to Satan. Even the coincidental pentagram layout from the five groups hasn't been linked to Satan."

McKay studied the carvings on the sides. They were all similar; humans kneeling, worshipping the creature on the top. He noticed the layout of the carving was such that the creature was sitting on something. A throne? Or a rock?

Preacher's Rock holds the secret. The last thing that woman had said to him was about this Preacher's Rock. McKay reached a hand out and tapped the box. It wasn't wood. It was solid stone. This stone had been carved and etched. The lettering was pristine.

"Let's open this up."

CHAPTER FIVE

Outside, the weather changed rapidly.

While it had started out a sunny, clear day, now the clouds rolled in.

Thunder rumbled, and lightning flashed across the sky.

The rain began to fall, picking up intensity as McKay examined the stone box.

McKay shouldn't have been surprised at the weight of the lid, but the stone's heft was far more than he expected. He lifted it up slowly, not sure what would be inside. When nothing flashed and no cloud billowed out, he flipped the lid over and laid it delicately on a file folder.

He saw that the lid had etchings on the underside, only visible now that it was exposed.

Аббадон, Могучий.

"What is that, Russian?"

While he waited for another translation, he let his fingertips run over the other markings. *Descendit procella,* this one read. *Latin again?*

There was one more etching, which McKay had seen before. It had been on the raised altar at the compound.

Отец возник.

"Somebody get me a fucking translation on this shit, right fucking now!"

McKay was sweating through his shirt, the moisture running down his sides, pooling at the top of his ass crack.

Finally, Officer Lickman held his phone out to McKay.

"Alright, let's see here. The Russian part reads '*Abbadon, the Mighty.*' Followed by '*blackness descends*' in Latin. And this last part, also in Russian. '*Father arise.*' So, if we read the front and back side as one sentence, we have a stone lid that reads '*For a new world would come. Abbadon, the Mighty. Blackness descends. Father arise.*' Jesus fucking Christ. What the fuck is this? Everybody out!"

Once the small office had been cleared and McKay was left alone, he slumped in his chair and stared at the carvings of the humans on their knees, arms outstretched. *Fucking sheep*, he thought.

Why is it always these mindless sheep? These people who should know better, who get hooked into these religious cults and then leave me a goddamned bloody mess to clean up after?

McKay didn't even want to look in the box. He'd caught a glimpse of a dark material, most likely a wooden box, when he'd opened the lid, but now he felt drained.

His hand throbbed where the nail had impaled him. He looked at the bandage, surprised to find no red tinge of leaking blood.

He was going to lean forward, build up some courage to dig deeper into the stone box, when the rain picked up in intensity, grabbing his attention.

McKay stood and looked outside. He hadn't even realized the weather had taken such a turn. He was pissed, as he'd planned on walking home. McKay smirked at the thought. He planned on walking home yesterday. He hadn't planned on spending the night or the ER trip, but now here he was. Going on thirty-six hours at the office.

A soft knock at the door stole his eyes from the window.

"Yeah?"

"McKay, sorry to do this man, but we got a call and Sarge says he needs you to do prelim on the scene. You won't be primary, but everyone else is out and they need a detective ASAP."

He looked at the box, then back to the cop.

"Fuck. OK. Give me a sec and I'll get the details from dispatch."

The box would have to wait.

He grabbed his jacket from the hanger on the back of the door, slipping it on. He flipped his light out, taking one last look at the carved stone on his desk, then closed the door behind him, making sure to test that it was locked.

WHEN HE FINALLY RETURNED TO the precinct the box was the furthest thing from his mind. He'd been at the scene far longer than expected, and after handing the keys to the officer at auto, he knew he needed to head home.

"I'm going to get some sleep," he muttered to the officer sitting at the nearest desk. "I'll get the paperwork done up later." The officer said something to him, but he was in a haze now, exhaustion finally grasping control of his brain.

McKay waved at the cop on duty at the intake desk, before stepping outside into the deluge from above. In his office he hadn't heard any thunder or lightning, but now outside the air hummed with the expectation of the next strike.

He'd always been anti-umbrella. Just the thought of holding a stick with a tent above his head made him grimace. On this walk home, he wished he was using one.

The drops were fat and solid, falling with enough speed to sting and make him wince a few times. He hadn't even crossed the street and he was soaked, his jacket offering little defense against the volume of liquid coming from the clouds.

The light changed and he briskly crossed, not wanting to run, but annoyed enough to speed walk.

McKay cut down through the alley between the Chinese food place and the Tattoo shop.

He was halfway down the span when he came to a halt.

It wasn't raining in the alley.

McKay looked to the clouds and saw the sky was still dark, but there was no rain falling here. There was nothing covering the alley or blocking the space.

For whatever reason, the rain wasn't coming down.

He decided not think too hard on this weather phenomena and just to keep hurrying home.

It was near the end of the far side of the alley that a noise caught his attention. He felt his palm begin to pulse, where the nail had invaded his flesh.

It was the sounds from an animal's hoof, clicking and clacking on the cement behind him.

McKay refused to turn. The sound behind him striking the deepest fear in his heart he'd ever experienced.

A new sound echoed, similar to nails on a chalkboard.

He knew then.

McKay knew if he turned, he'd come face to face with the horned beast that was on the lid of the stone box. It would be ten feet tall, two massive horns curling from its goat head. It would be dragging its clawed hands against each building on either side of the alley, walking purposefully towards the detective.

He could even hear it breathing, the snort and huff from its snout.

When the sound stopped mere feet behind him, the rain began again.

McKay ran faster than he'd ever run in his life when the creature behind him whispered *'Father arise.'*

CHAPTER SEVEN

He flopped onto his bed and let his arms splay out to his sides. He stared at the ceiling fan spinning around as it *whomped whomped* slowly.

McKay kicked his shoes off. He was drenched from the storm, which was still raging outside.

Now that he was home, McKay felt foolish.

Fucking overactive imagination, he told himself. *Too many long days without sleep.*

There had been nothing in that alley. It had been a cat. Someone had tossed some garbage out from a store. He kept running these scenarios through his mind, but he knew for certain there had been no demon stalking him. The rain had kept falling, it was just his eyes playing tricks on him.

He flexed his hand, wincing with how sore it was. That piece of rusted metal had done a number on his palm. McKay wasn't too fond of the tetanus shot he'd had either.

I need to change out of these wet clothes, he thought, *turn off that fucking fan.*

Exhaustion won.

The storm grew as his eyes fell heavy and he drifted off to sleep.

Outside, on the grass, a figure pointed towards his darkened window.

CHAPTER EIGHT

McKay woke with a start, covered in sweat and still unnerved from his trip home. He was breathing heavily; his dream frightening but immediately forgotten once his eyes popped open.

The room was pitch black, the storm outside continuing even as night arrived.

He found his cell phone on the nightstand and pushed the side button, the screen illuminating.

9:00 pm.

Jesus, I've slept for almost twelve hours, he realized.

McKay saw some text notifications and a few missed calls. One jogged his memory. Missed call from Freddy. That'd be about the mystery woman. They could all wait. His body was telling him that he needed to piss and then crawl back into bed, this time under the sheets. More sleep was on the agenda.

He sat up and stared at the far side of the room.

It was immeasurably black. Normally his dresser sat

there. Even at night the hardware on each drawer would reflect some of the light from the street lights outside.

Everything churned when he realized that within the black, a figure was materializing.

"Who's there?" he asked. His voice cracked, and he sounded defeated in a way he'd never believed possible before.

The room shifted before him, the void fading away, returning his room to its normal configuration. The corner was still dark, but McKay knew someone was sitting there.

"McKay," a husky voice replied. He recognized it immediately as the woman who'd assaulted him.

"How'd you get in here?"

"An attractive woman is in your room and that's your question?"

"You stabbed me and broke my nose last time," he replied.

She laughed, the sound forcing his dick to twitch. It was the sound of someone you've just paid to fuck and they now saw you as the most charming person ever. While his bottom half betrayed him, his mind was racing. This wasn't good. He needed to get his revolver from his nightstand.

"I'm not here to kill you, McKay. I'm here to open your mind and give you more insight into what you've been thrust into."

She stood, her red silk dress falling away from her curvy figure.

McKay was losing the battle. Her aroma, even from a distance, was intoxicating.

The air bristled.

She was now standing directly before him, and just as

quick as she'd impaled him, she grabbed his head and pushed it between her breasts.

He'd lost the battle.

She pushed him back, his fall to the mattress making him feel like he was as light as a feather. Instead of taking off his pants, McKay watched her crawl up his body until she straddled his chest.

"You were never meant to be a part of this. Now, you've begun to ask questions about an incident where no answers can be found. You will learn more about events in the past when you examine that package in your office. For now, let's give you a taste of what you've stumbled upon."

She put one knee on either side of his head and before he could resist, McKay felt her pussy smash into his mouth. His tongue eagerly started to lick, his teeth and lips nibbling her folds. Her pubic hair pressed into his nose, which he breathed deeply. McKay didn't know what he expected, but the smell was earthy and invigorating. As she rode his face harder and faster, she began to moan and tremble. His nose throbbed and ached, the mangled cartilage screaming at the pressure.

McKay felt a gush of fluid spurting forth from her. It was thick and filled his mouth, flowing onto his chin and cheeks. He was expecting it to be sweet or ammonia tinted, but instead he recognized the metallic bite of blood. He struggled to push her off, but she was too strong, and instead she began to grind his face harder.

She grabbed his hair, and while she pushed down harder, she pulled his head upwards. He was locked into place. But for some reason, he kept licking.

His eyes burst wide when he felt it.

A new weight had joined them on the bed. McKay

couldn't see anything because this nude goddess was on his face.

Then he heard a gruff breath. His zipper was lowered and his pants undone. They were roughly yanked down his legs, his cock bobbing around once exposed.

Before he could try and kick this unseen intruder, McKay felt his dick engulfed into their mouth and when it bit down on the base of his shaft, a bright light exploded through his head.

Proverbs 27:20
*Hell and Destruction are never full; so the eyes of man are
never satisfied.*

1929

CHAPTER NINE

Father stood before his congregation, smiling.

He now knew the truth. The beast had told him to collect some of the discarded remains when Preacher's Rock had exploded.

Looking at the headless bodies before him, his cheeks ached from how hard he smiled.

The black veil had been lifted from his eyes.

Ascension was possible. He'd seen it when he collected the stone.

The black heavens were *above* and *beyond*.

Here and *there*.

In order to go forth and complete the ritual, he'd require a new flock.

This time one dedicated to the cause. It was clear from Nathaniel's failure that they were not pure of sin.

He'd begin recruiting in the morning.

Until then, he had to start carving the stone, forming it into its true purpose.

CHAPTER TEN

The thing Father always found interesting about humans, was that as a whole the majority were unintelligent. So, when a man wearing a robe walked into town, asking the people on the sidewalks if they had a moment to discuss religion, it only took him three days and he had one hundred new members that were planning on moving to the base of Preacher's Rock by the weekend.

He was exhilarated, when he returned to the complex.

To prepare for their arrival, he needed to dispose of all of the remains still scattered around the grounds.

While the bodies had been stacked and burned from the area near the campfire, the beast had also beheaded the parishioners who had remained in their tents and huts.

Once every residence had been cleaned and blessed, Father felt a weight leave his chest.

He would greet them one by one.

He would catalog all of the men, women and children.

Then he would choose a man and a woman to fulfill his needs and begin the next phase towards immortality.

CHAPTER ELEVEN

I t had been a month since the compound had been re-
populated.

While the initial few weeks had seen some growing
pains, Father was now pleased with how well the group inter-
acted. They all had learned their jobs, their new roles.

Leaving your old life behind was tough, he knew, but for
the betterment of their chances to transcend the black realm
and join their gods above, each person needed to accept their
position and do it with vigor.

EACH NIGHT, after final prayer and the group had dispersed
back to their sleeping quarters, Father would retrieve a
lantern and his walking stick and make the quarter mile hike
to the base of Preacher's Rock.

The instructions had been clear. He needed to follow
them to the exact specifications if he was to achieve his ulti-
mate goal.

He was ready to determine who would need to take his seed, who would carry his child. For this to occur the stars would tell him through his sacrifice.

On this night, he sat at the base of a leafless tree and silently cut eleven thin strips of skin from the inside of his thighs. Once they had all been removed, he laid them on a flat rock before him, and meditated while looking to the sky.

After some time, his eyes lit up as the stars twinkled in such a way that he knew it was a message. He closed his eyes and let the beast speak to him.

He picked up ten of the pieces and swallowed them whole.

Turning the eleventh piece over he stared at the thin lines of blood left behind.

They spelled out a name.

He smiled as he stood, his thighs stinging from the wounds.

As he returned back to the compound, the blood made a squelching noise as he shuffled along.

The sensation of the fluid dripping down his legs made him harder than he'd been in some time.

For the next week, Father watched her.

When they had Morning Prayer, afternoon study and danced around the fire at night, he watched.

He'd sit off to the side, one hand tucked under his robe, slowly moving it along the rough skin of his penis. He knew he needed to walk that fine line for the rest of the week. He needed to be close, edged to the extreme so that when their union was consummated, the gods above and below would experience his release.

The men all clapped as the women danced and circled the flickering fire light. Her eyes caught his as she came around, and she smiled.

Father caught the red glow within her, saw her blonde hair twirl and fall, and knew the time was upon him when the clawed hand rested on his shoulder.

CHAPTER TWELVE

The next day, Father led them in their Morning Prayer. He conducted a sermon where he focused on helping thy fellow neighbour and ensuring that each member went above and beyond to fulfill the prophecy.

He'd yet to fully explain to them what they would attempt to be doing. He didn't want to overwhelm the group.

Soon they'd need to understand that they served a higher purpose.

While he spoke, he made sure to make direct eye contact with her. She smiled and licked her lips slowly, pulling her bottom lip in a bit and biting it with her teeth.

Father had no doubts now. The stars had spoken that evening.

To him and to her.

CHAPTER THIRTEEN

He approached her that afternoon, watching her coyly catch his gaze, smile then look away. Her beauty was ageless. A man as holy as he should find no attraction for procreation, yet she pushed him to toss away his ideals.

He took her hand, pulled her close, pressed his engorged groin into her stomach.

"Lily," he whispered, her head buried in his long, grey beard.

"Yes, my love," she replied, moving her hand lower to grab him.

"The heavens I crave have spoken to me. They've signalled that it is you to bring forth a child."

"I know, my love. The horned one has spoken to me, in my dreams."

This surprised the man. He hadn't expected her to be receptive.

"Tonight, we meet."

He shoved her down, watching her face change from lust to shock as she hit the ground.

Father spun and departed, not caring if her feelings had been hurt.

He wasn't making love to a woman. He was fulfilling his duty to bring the opening one step closer.

CHAPTER FOURTEEN

As dusk arrived, she was summoned.

She followed a fire-lit path through the desert, leading away from the compound.

The sky was clear, which helped lower her anxiety.

She stepped forth from the path into a small clearing at the base of a hill. She knew this hill used to be home to Preacher's Rock at the summit.

Now, she found Father standing before her, candles lit in a circle around him.

He stood nude, his body frail, his inner thighs bloody.

His member bobbed before him. Red, swollen and fixated on her.

Father wore a mask that covered his face from the nose up.

One long horn protruded from his forehead and extended back behind his head. Two tusks sprouted from each cheek and came to a point before his face.

"Lily, come. Please."

She walked within arms distance, calmer than expected.

So close to Father now, she was shocked at how little there was of him. The robe he wore disguised his skeletal figure beneath. She could see his ribs protruding, and his skin was thin to the point of being translucent. Blue veins crossed over most of his tissue.

Father took her hand and squeezed it, smiling at her from below the mask.

He deftly reached out and slipped her robe off, leaving her nude.

She kneeled before him, keeping her eyes fixed on his, the mask shrouding them. As she went to take him in her mouth, he pushed her away.

She fell back, parting her legs. As he knelt down between them, the candles all snuffed out and around the area she now heard snorts and grunts.

As Father entered her, thrusting hard, she heard steps come closer, and saw the glint of eyes within the night.

The gods were watching.

She raised her knees, letting the old man pound deeper, and when she looked at the moon and saw it flicker and go black, she knew he was about to climax.

Father confirmed her thought with a guttural noise. His cock thickened, threatening to split her from the inside. The pain was terrifyingly desired. She watched in horror as his face distorted, taking the form of the beast on the mask. His chest and arms grew wide and darkened, thick fur sprouting before disappearing.

As he finished spurting deep within, he returned to his shrivelled state, the mask falling from his head, clanging against the dirt ground.

A voice spoke from the dark, *"It is done."*

The candles danced back to life and she found that

Father stood before her, his robe back on and his walking stick in one hand.

"The consecration has occurred. You will be bathed and lathered in the days and months until the arrival. Please, follow me."

He helped her to her feet and she was surprised that none of his seed leaked out. It was as though an internal presence had lapped it up, absorbed it as soon as it entered her.

She walked behind him, nude and sore.

When they returned to the complex, two women met them, covered her in a thin robe, and led her to a hut near Father's sleeping quarters.

Once she entered, Father made his way to an area he kept hidden from the others, a small alcove behind the chapel.

There he disrobed, grabbed a cat-o-nine tails, and began to whip himself across his back and sides as he prayed for forgiveness for the act he'd committed, and for what was to come.

CHAPTER FIFTEEN

She could feel it grow and develop immediately.

Nothing was natural about her pregnancy. Within weeks, her stomach grew and bulged and before long she could feet the patter of little feet kicking her insides.

Father only came to visit once a week, and when he did, he wouldn't make eye contact. He would ask the midwives how things were progressing, and leave.

Each day was the same routine. Her stomach was slathered in lotions and creams and she was fed better than the group.

At night she heard the sound of a knife being sharpened on a whetstone.

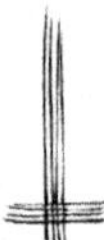

CHAPTER SIXTEEN

Three months from conception, Lily woke in agony.

She screamed in pain as the little one in her stomach bashed and crashed, determined to make its way to the outside world.

"It's time," a female's voice said.

Lily looked over and saw a woman shrouded in a hooded robe.

She'd never seen this woman before.

"Who are you? What are you doing here?" Lily demanded, but fell silent when an immense figure loomed over their shoulder.

She couldn't make out its details, just a shape, but she knew this was one of the beasts that had watched Father and her under the rock.

Two more hooded women joined them, and as Lily was held down, Father entered her sleeping area.

He never made eye contact with Lily, instead retrieving the knife that had been sharpened nightly, and ran it across both of his palms. As the blood began to leak from his hands, he knelt, and before she could react, slid the knife across her lower abdomen. As her amniotic sac flopped out, the child still within, Father smeared the congealed mixture of fluids and tissue all over his face.

A noise beside her grabbed her attention. She glanced to her right and as she did, felt a stabbing pain in the middle of her forehead as a nail was impaled into her frontal lobe.

The tiny redheaded child grew big and strong quickly. Her assigned midwives and wet nurses made sure she was cared for and nurtured.

They kept Lily in a tent near the back of the complex, away from the other residents. She wandered the hillside behind the community for years, mouth open and drool dribbling down the sides of her chin.

Her eyes never focused, never locked onto a specific thing.

Father had no remorse or guilt over her earthly vegetative state.

He knew she'd already ascended to the black heavens.

Her role in creating their daughter was complete.

Her reward was immortality in the cosmos.

Job 10:22
The land of gloom and chaos,
Where light is like darkness.

McKay screamed back into consciousness.

He looked around his bedroom, finding it bright, the sun shining outside.

The storm had moved on.

McKay expected to see the redheaded woman still sitting in the chair in the corner.

Instead he was alone.

His hand throbbed in agony, his head pounding from the punishment his nose and face had received over the last few days.

McKay sat on the edge of the bed, covered in his blanket. He didn't want to take the blanket off. He knew below would be *things* he didn't want to see or accept.

There were different aches and pains, but the part he was struggling with the most was his rational mind. None of this should be possible.

McKay counted to three in his head, and pulled the blanket aside.

His thighs were cut to shreds. He could see where skin

had been peeled back and removed, the muscle gleaming below. Eleven strips missing.

While his cock was still attached to his body, deep, dark bite wounds surrounded the base of his shaft and his balls were covered in blood. He was surprised that they still hung below, as the pain made him believe they'd been removed.

McKay found his footing and dared to stand. The room spun for a moment, but nothing worse than a few of the nights he'd drank himself into a stupor.

He shuffled to the bathroom, forcing himself to flick on the light and wait for his eyes to adjust to the brightness. Once done, he stepped before the mirror to look at the monster staring back at him.

His nose was pushed to one side, the nostrils packed with darkened, dried blood accompanied with fresh, running through it.

His lips, chin and cheeks were also caked with dark redness.

McKay didn't have a clue how he'd get cleaned up. He couldn't step into the shower to let the water wash it all away, it would sting and burn his eviscerated thighs. But he also couldn't wash his face off with one bandaged hand. The pain that any pressure would cause would be off the charts. He was fucked either way. So, he rummaged through his drawers, finding two elastic tensor bandages. McKay wrapped them around each thigh; tight but gentle. After that was done, he twisted the shower knob and waited until the water had warmed up to a tolerable heat. He stepped in with his back facing the spray, then slowly turned, allowing his face to get used to some of the pressure from the water.

It was excruciating at first, but after some time, he let the water cascade over his broken-down body. The tensor wraps did their jobs, with only a few moments of stinging pain. He wet a washcloth and delicately used it to scrub the dried blood from the rest of his face, leaving his nose for the shower nozzle alone.

McKay had to step out of the shower twice to look at his face, only to return and let the water rinse away more blood.

Finally, with only some dried gobs still around his nostrils, he turned the water off and used a towel to dry himself. He took his time on his face, dabbing and wincing as he went. He'd not bothered to wash his hair, but the motion of moving the towel back and forth on his scalp caused his eyes to water as his nose was jostled.

Once dry, he left the washroom and returned to sitting on his bed. He knew he should go back to emergency, get a once over and his legs stitched up, but the vision he'd seen when that lady had forced herself on his face was too much to ignore. McKay hadn't expected to learn what he'd learned, and he had to inspect that box sitting on his office desk more.

It was then that he saw the wall across from his bed. Last night it had been a large black void, but now in its normal state of just being a wall, long, thick scratch marks covered it from floor to ceiling.

In the middle, carved out in thick block letters, was one word.

FATHER.

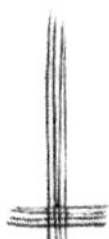

It took McKay a considerable amount of time to get dressed. He decided to change the wet tensor wraps on his legs, replacing them with clean, dry ones. When he'd undone the first one, he found it hurt like fuck to take it off, the sticky gore below clinging to the bandage.

Once he deemed his appearance acceptable, he called for a cab and waited in front of his place. McKay didn't smoke, but a part of him wished he did, longing for something in his hand, something to relax him.

He kept scanning the area, looking at the bushes and shadows nearby, expecting to see something hiding in wait.

"Hey, fella? You call for a cab?"

The cab driver startled him, so lost in thought and worry that he hadn't even heard it pull up.

The man honked now, frustration showing.

"Yeah. Yes, sorry," he said, trying to walk normally to the cab.

It hurt getting into the low vehicle, having to bend down and slide over on the seat.

When he got dropped off in front of the precinct, the officers outside of the building saw him and hustled over, helping him get out of the cab.

"Jesus, McKay? What the fuck happened?"

"You wouldn't believe me," he replied, making his way to his office.

He felt every set of eyes on him as he shuffled across the work floor.

McKay struggled to get the office unlocked, then when successful, pushed the door open and had to step back.

A smell like rot and sulphur exploded out, causing the officers nearby to rush and open the windows.

"Didn't smell like that when you left," one mentioned.

"No, no it did not."

CHAPTER TWENTY

McKay shut the door behind him and sat at his desk, his chair feeling infinitely more comfortable than the cab seat had been.

He needed some time to process the events thus far. Catalog what he could. Make notes. Procedural stuff. He was still struggling with how implausible this entire thing seemed. McKay needed to focus on the normal, the mundane and routine.

Since Kramer had decided to take his own life, it had been one odd occurrence after another and if there was one thing a career of being a detective had taught him, it was to look for the pattern.

So, ignoring the box and the stench permeating the air, McKay went to his large white board and wiped it clean. He started off at the top, jotting down what he had seen in the vision. Father at the top, then Lilly, followed by the redhead child with an arrow to the right and the words 'mystery woman' beside it.

Below, he made two branches; the first for Abaddon, he'd

need to research this. He put in a call for someone to get a biblical expert to come immediately. The second branch was for Brad. He didn't understand how this random male – one that through interviews he'd determined was quite possibly the most boring man in the world – had been deemed a chosen figure to lead a ritual.

By the time he'd made a few inconsequential other notes, a knock on the door got his attention.

Turning he saw a man who looked similar to himself. Late 40's to early 50's. Tailored suit, grey black hair combed to one side.

"Can I help you?"

"I'm Professor Bianchi. I received a call and was instructed that a Detective McKay had some questions in an investigation regarding a biblical issue?"

"Fuck. That was fast."

"I was actually just down the street leaving court where I'd been testifying as an expert witness. Two-minute walk."

McKay nodded, and motioned at the chair across his desk.

"Please, sit."

The professor sat and set his briefcase on his lap, which he popped open and pulled out a slim laptop. It was only then that he spotted the stone box on the desk before him. His face dropped, eyes growing wide, coloring disappearing.

"Where the fuck did you get Abaddon's heart?"

McKay just stared at the man. He'd gone from together and professional to undone in moments. He'd not expected that from a man who'd been called as an expert witness.

"Abaddon's heart?"

"Abaddon is both a place and an entity. A bottomless pit but also the king of the locusts. The bringer of plagues.

Abaddon is often accompanied by Sheol – also a place and an entity."

Sheol. McKay made a note on the whiteboard, referencing the group that had opened fire while chanting that word.

"Interestingly, the name has a number of translations. The entity has been referred to as 'the destroyer,' 'the angel of death' as well as 'doom' or 'to perish.' This entity has also been linked to the prophecy of 'The Black Heavens.' In some cult sects, the black heavens are the astrological or cosmic location of immortality."

Now McKay's own expression change. This professor seemed to be giving him all of the information he needed, without even being prompted. Normally he'd be suspicious of something like this, but after what he'd experienced, he knew better.

"So, Abaddon's heart is what?"

Bianchi leaned in closer, examining the sides of the stone as well as the lid on top. Even though his initial reaction had been deep fear, he was nevertheless showing excitement over what was sitting before him.

"Sorry, would you mind if I took some pictures of this? This is extraordinary to just stumble on this in person."

"Have at it. There's something under the lid I can show you when you're done on the outside. Then can you answer me?"

"Yes, yes," he said, quickly retrieving his cellphone and pulling up the camera app.

Once he was done taking his photos of the side and top, McKay flipped the lid over and let him inspect the under surface. He purposefully blocked the box inside. He hadn't yet inspected this and didn't want to disclose something unintentionally.

"OK, all done?"

Bianchi nodded, returning to the seat.

"Alright, Abaddon's heart. In my circles you hear stories within the collector's world, the black market of artifacts. A number of us who are... more open to working within this world of collector's, know of its origins. The story goes that Abaddon, was banished to the underworld. While there, the entity was slain by the sword of an unknown soldier. The heart was removed and placed inside a box."

He stopped here and eyed McKay. McKay realized Bianchi had been expecting to be interrupted. The subject matter was such that he'd probably been interrupted before.

"Well, we hear nothing of the box for some time. There are rumblings of it being used in various rituals, or of many of the immoral Popes using it to speak to God, but it just disappears from the record. Sure, we see some documents suggesting it was transported to Russia where the mad monk, Rasputin was privy to it. Some believe he successfully contacted Abaddon, and he himself ascended to the black heavens."

This would explain the languages on the box, McKay thought.

"Is that the end of the story?" McKay asked.

"No. We get some time again where information goes dark. The last I'd heard of the box was that it was seen in France. So, from France, to your desk. Now, here it sits."

McKay had to sit and stare at the box before him. While he couldn't fathom all that Bianchi stated, it did paint a vivid picture. One that he could see related to this Father character, who was so hell bent on this prophecy and promise of immortality he'd do whatever it took.

"What is the purpose of all of this? Of the Abaddon heart?"

"Detective. The purpose is that it is a direct line to Abaddon. That what is stored in the box not only relates to the entity as well as the location, but that it also allows communication with the beast. That is, if the ritual is done correctly and favour is received."

"Favour?"

"Yes. An entity such as Abaddon is something that will only do something in return. A favour for a favour. A ritual must be performed. The documents I've seen have all said that those who've tried to summon this beast have had to ensure every single thing is done perfectly, and without pause or fail, for Abaddon to be pleased and to open up the black void. Allow a human to step into the black heavens."

McKay felt his blood run cold. *Black void? Like in his bedroom?*

"May I ask a question, Detective McKay?"

McKay nodded, unsure what would be asked.

"Is there a wooden box within this stone box?"

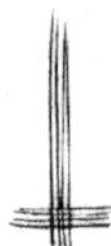

McKay didn't want to answer the man. He wanted none of this to be happening. Hearing all of this backstory, his thighs throbbed and his hand itched.

"There is."

Bianchi nodded.

The two sat silently, contemplating what that meant.

Finally, Bianchi took the lead.

"Have you looked inside?"

"I have not."

"May I ask, is this box related to your appearance?"

"It is."

"I think, for me to have a better understanding of what my role can be for you, I'd like you to fill me in please."

McKay filled him in.

On everything.

Starting from his deceased partner going to visit Father and his flock, up until Bianchi had knocked on his office door. He left nothing out, not even the visit by the woman and the events that occurred. McKay told him every detail he could of the vision, and even what had happened to him physically.

It felt good to get it off of his chest, but at the same time he was now concerned about Bianchi leaking any of these details.

Once done, Bianchi took a few minutes. He stared at the stone again, hands together.

"I think for me to help at all, the next step would be for me to sign an NDA."

"A non-disclosure agreement?"

"Yes. I need to make sure you are completely honest with me. Someone in your position will be worried that I might take the info and run. We need to trust each other. We need to open that box and for you to know that I will not share anything that we've discussed. I would, however, like to email these photos to a trusted colleague to get their opinion on what it is we are looking at. I'm very confident, but a second opinion is best."

"Absolutely. Go ahead. I'll get that NDA here within ten minutes."

McKay made a call and then the two waited for it to arrive.

Both knew that once Bianchi signed the document, they'd open up the box.

CHAPTER TWENTY-TWO

Outside a new storm moved in.

The sky was dark and angry.

The clouds opened and the rain drops began slamming to the ground.

People walking along the sidewalks took cover.

At first, they thought it was just rain, but the buzzing of locusts in the distance created a fear all on its own.

CHAPTER TWENTY-THREE

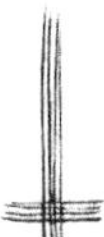

Once Bianchi signed the forms, McKay opened his bottom drawer, took out two shot glasses and put them on the desk. He grabbed a small bottle from the drawer, filled both glasses, and replaced the bottle.

McKay handed one to the professor and lifted the other before him.

They touched glasses and drank the liquor in one shot.

Once the glasses were set to the side, McKay got up and closed the office door, and flipped the blinds closed.

"Shall we?"

Bianchi nodded.

McKay found he was breathing heavy, sweat dripping down his forehead and stinging his eyes and nose.

His nose had thankfully stopped bleeding, but the little cuts and scrapes let him know it was still as fucked up as he remembered it.

Every time he moved, he grimaced.

The two stood, staring down at the stone box.

The beast carved in the top stared back, almost daring them to go down this rabbit hole.

McKay handed Bianchi some gloves, while putting his on.

The two shared one more look, before McKay grasped the lid and pulled it off, setting it on the cabinet against the side wall.

"You haven't looked at anything in here yet?"

"No. I couldn't bring myself to do it before. Exhaustion. Fear. Not sure, but I had to wait."

"Fair enough," Bianchi replied. "How about I'll take photos and catalog each piece as you take things out? That way at least there's some formality to this process?"

"That works."

McKay took a cursory glance inside to see what was there. He reached in and took out the wooden box first. He'd almost expected a shock or a pain to occur when he made contact, but was thankful nothing happened.

"First item is a wooden box," he said to the professor. "I'd say it's eight inches deep by eight inches wide. Maybe ten inches long? There are markings on it, but the wood is too dark to see. I'll get forensics to lighten it up."

He set it beside Bianchi, who began taking pictures. Once he was done, he nodded and McKay reached in again.

"Second item is a thick Manilla envelope. Something is inside. Envelope is nine inches across by maybe a foot tall. With the stuff inside, I'd wager its three inches thick."

He set this on the desk for Bianchi to catalog.

He looked in again and saw there were two more objects. One caught his eye more than the other. He pulled it out and saw Bianchi's eyes go wide.

"Item number is three is a roll of film. Not sure of type.

Old. Looks like we'll need a projector to watch it. There is a date on the side. Very faded. It may say June or July, but the year is visible. 1979."

He set it down for Bianchi, and reached in, grabbing the last object. He pulled it out and saw it was a black sack. It had a pull cord to tighten at the top, and the material was soft and smooth. It didn't feel like leather, but was close.

"Last item. Not sure what this is. Carrying sack? There is something inside but it isn't heavy."

He set it down and Bianchi quickly snapped some more pictures on his phone.

"OK. Now let's go through each item. Let's start with the box."

McKay pulled it over and examined the outside. It looked like there were letters etched into the sides, but someone either had polished the exterior or age had distorted it. He'd let forensics deal with it.

He flipped the lid open and stared at what greeted him.

"Fuck."

Bianchi covered his mouth after swearing.

Inside the wooden box were two six-inch-long horns.

"Those can't be real, can they?"

Bianchi was talking to himself now. He stood and paced his side of the desk, muttering to himself.

McKay gently removed them both, setting them on the desk. The ends were smooth, as though they had been cut off of whatever they'd belonged to.

"The horns look like they start to curve but they were removed just before that point."

McKay heard Bianchi, but he blocked most of it out.

"Let's look in this envelope."

He unlooped the red thread that kept the envelope closed.

Once it was undone, he looked inside, not surprised to find a stack of photos.

Some were in black-and-white, while others were in color.

McKay saw that they were in some semblance of an order, so he started at the top of the stack, and analyzed each one before passing it to Bianchi, who'd now returned to sitting.

The first fifty or so photos were mundane. Boring to a degree. All were in black-and-white and all appeared to be showing daily life at the compound.

Some showed women doing laundry or making food, some showed them playing with children or teaching them various things. There were photos of them all kneeling and looking forward, McKay assumed this was them praying or attending their church. Other photos showed men making and building things, shirtless and sweaty. It spoke to the time period, McKay realized. Of women doing female chores and men doing male tasks. Most cults seemed to want to maintain that patriarchal mentality. This was similar to most religions.

It wasn't until fifty or so pictures in that McKay experienced a sharp kick to his stomach. The photo before him showed Father, standing beside a very pregnant woman. He knew that was Lily. He hadn't seen much in his vision of things like this, but he knew the vision had served a purpose. It was unsettling to look upon them as a 'couple.' They looked happy even.

The next few photos showed Father in various moments; a man knelt before him, Father touching his head with his eyes closed. Father standing on a rock above the gathered crowd, arms wide.

It wasn't until the photos turned to color that the content began to change.

Gone were the mundane scenes of life. Instead, McKay was looking at true horror.

The first photo showed a woman with blood covering her hands sitting under a tree. Beside her sat what McKay assumed were intestines. He wasn't sure as the photo was blurry, but the ropey viscera possessed a distinct shape, one McKay had seen far too many times on the job. A body hung from a branch beside where she sat, their stomach splayed open and empty.

In the next one, Father stood nude while a man was kneeling before him. Father held a hammer high above the man. In the next photo, a man lay on the ground with a bloody hammer sticking out of his skull.

The next few photos displayed some men and women nude. Each were bound to a wooden cross. Long, red marks criss-crossed their fronts and backs. Father stood near them with a whip in his hand.

It was evident from the photos that Father was becoming more and more depraved and hurtful. Angry.

It was near the back of the stack that McKay found the most interesting photos. Some were showing a circle of candles in the dirt, Father standing with his robe pulled open, long cuts bleeding on his chest.

Others showed a robed man, wearing a mask with horns, pouring red liquid from a cup over crying babies.

These images got to McKay. He'd seen a lot of fucked up shit in his career, experienced things and witnessed events that humans shouldn't. Even the visit hadn't affected him like this. These innocent children were simply playthings in Father's quest for immortality.

He set the photos aside, giving himself a breather. He asked Bianchi if he wanted a coffee, and excused himself to get them each a cup.

When he returned, Bianchi was still jotting down notes related to each photo before him.

"Thanks," the professor said, taking a sip before setting it on the desk.

McKay picked the stack up, feeling a bit better.

The next few photos were startling.

While out of focus and blurry, as though the photographer was either moving or trying to be stealthy, they each showed something McKay didn't believe he'd ever see.

The first was a photo of a woman strapped to a chair. She was covered in blood. Father stood to her side, holding a knife. Behind the chair, at the edge of the darkness, was the outline of a large figure. McKay could swear that he could see red eyes, hooves, and twisted horns on top of its head.

The next few were similar. A male bound nude over a log, Father pressed up behind the man, robe thrown back. The male's head had a clawed hand placed on it, the owner of the hand just off camera.

McKay handed these to Bianchi and waited for the man to get to them. When he did, he jumped up, chair pushed back, toppling over and hitting the ground.

"It can't be," he said, pointing at the picture.

The professor crossed himself and exited the office, walking across the work floor without looking back.

While he waited for his return, McKay flipped through the last dozen photos. These were simple ones, nothing really of note. It was a stark change in subject matter. Members all dancing around a campfire, a woman sitting with a few children.

The last photo caught his attention.

It was a Polaroid.

It was of two boys and a girl sitting at a table. The first boy was young, maybe five. The second boy was younger still, maybe two. The girl was older, she looked to be a teenager.

The date said "May 13th, 1992."

McKay felt his heart race when he stared at the girl. He knew her. It clicked into place that it was the mystery woman who had assaulted him.

The name of the girl was smudged and unreadable.

The younger of the two had nothing written under him.

The name written under the older boy was easy to read.

Brad, age five.

McKay looked in the envelope and found a piece of discarded paper left behind. Pulling it out, he read what was written on it.

'Watch the film.'

Psalm 143:3
For the enemy has pursued me,
crushing my life to the ground,
making me sit in darkness like those long dead.

It was as though the note in the envelope was speaking to McKay from beyond.

He sent a request for a video technician, someone who could figure out what type of film was on this reel and get a projector to broadcast it.

McKay contacted a colleague in another precinct to come watch.

With any video found of this nature, he wanted to ensure that what was seen the first time would not be doctored and manipulated if this was to be used in court. This way his colleague could verify the authenticity of what was shown on the film. They'd send it to forensics to have someone verify the age, and that the film hadn't been altered after viewing it.

While they waited for McKay's colleague to arrive and the projector to be set up, they decided to order some food. Both were starving, not having realized how much of the day had gotten away from them.

After deciding on pizza, McKay was surprised when the guy at the pizza joint said it would take an hour to deliver.

"You haven't seen the storm outside?" he asked, his voice bordering on annoyance.

"No, sorry. I've been inside all day investigating a homicide."

McKay chuckled when the guy apologized and said he'd try and speed the food up. That line always got civilians.

He hit End Call and sat down, feeling the weight of everything climbing up his shoulders.

"Fuck me, I'm tired."

"You look it, no offense," Bianchi said, as he kept typing on his laptop.

McKay waved it off.

"Gonna piss."

Leaving the office, his thighs screamed with the exertion, his hand howling when he opened and closed it.

When all of this is over, I'm gonna need a massage, he thought. *A nice happy ending to relieve some stress.*

McKay pushed the door as he entered the washroom, cringing as it creaked.

He walked to the urinal, unzipped and let out a sigh as his bladder emptied.

It was then that he heard a snort and smelled rotting flesh.

He closed his eyes, finished peeing, then zipped up slowly.

McKay turned, washed his hands and then walked as fast as he could out of the washroom. He almost bumped into an officer entering, who said *watch it,* as he entered and McKay left.

He didn't hear anything. No screams of agony or sounds of a struggle.

Making his way back to his office, he found his colleague standing at the doorway waiting for him.

When Detective Grant turned and saw McKay, he didn't hide his shock.

"You weren't kidding when you said he was fucked up," Grant said to Bianchi.

"Real joker," McKay replied, grabbing a chair from an officer's desk and positioning it for Grant.

The tech arrived, quickly determining what type of film it was, and set it up on the projector.

"Good to go, McKay. Just call when you're done and I'll break the equipment down and catalog the reel."

The man left, leaving the three sitting in the office.

"You want more background on this, Grant? Other than it's related to the cult?"

"Nah. Let's go in blind."

McKay nodded, turned off the light, and flipped the switch on the side.

The machine made a clacking noise, before whirling to life.

A picture emerged on the projector screen on the far wall.

One McKay and Bianchi couldn't believe.

There was no sound.

The room was silent other than the whirl of the projector.

Outside the rain continued to increase in intensity.

The thunder rumbled, the lightning beginning to flash and strike.

A shrouded figure strode from between two buildings, and then stood outside on the lawn of the precinct.

They began to chant '*Sheol, Sheol,*' over and over again.

As the picture came into focus in the office and the three men saw the first image of Father sitting before the camera, the figure removed their robe.

Standing naked in the rain, they dropped to their knees, arms stretched above them.

A second figure emerged from the alley, walked briskly to the nude person and slit their throat.

They disappeared back into the blackness before any one even noticed they'd been there.

CHAPTER TWENTY-SIX

McKay, Grant and Bianchi heard a commotion outside the office, but ignored it. The film had flickered to life, Father sitting before the camera.

With no sound, it was irritating to be unable to hear what he was saying, but from what they could see it appeared he was reading something out loud.

"Who's this guy?" Grant asked.

"Father. Head of the cult."

"Whack job," Grant chuckled.

The camera angle was such that Father appeared to be addressing people behind the setup, but the camera never turned to show any group of gathered people.

It flickered and a new scene began.

This one was immediately shocking.

It showed a group of naked worshippers wearing masks, all crawling in circles on their hands and knees. As they passed Father, he would whip them, kick them or slash at them with an object. By the third trip around the man, the parishioners were bloody and even with no sound, one could see they were screaming in pain.

"Some kinky shit you two are watching," Grant said, laughing.

A new scene came on.

This one showed Father sodomizing a male. He was pumping rigorously into the male's rear while he burned the man's back with a torch he was holding. The area around them was dark, not visible to the camera, but it was within that blackness that Bianchi spotted something.

"What the fuck is that?"

He was pointing to a place on the screen to the top right.

In the area, McKay and Grant both started to see what Bianchi had spotted. Something immense and disfigured was swaying in and out of the shadows.

"Is that fucking nut job wearing a dead goats head? Perv's man," Grant joked.

"No. We believe what we are seeing is real footage of Abaddon," Bianchi replied.

"Abaddon? Like a fucking demon?"

"Entity," Bianchi was quick to point out.

"It's a fucking demon," Grant replied.

The three men watched. The faster and harder Father fucked that tortured male, the closer and closer the creature came to stepping into the light.

"I've watched enough porn to know that old man's about to blow his load," Grant said, leaning in and staring at the blackness before the creature.

"Come on, motherfucker. Step into the light." Grant was sitting right on the edge of his seat now.

On screen, Father thrust into the man one last time, then

threw his head back. From this angle, they could see he was in ecstasy.

"There it is! Holy fucking shit!"

Grant was practically jumping out of his chair as the creature stepped from the shadows.

Fully exposed, McKay inhaled hard, Bianchi matching his shock.

The creature was easily ten feet tall, filling up the side of the screen. It was standing on two hairy legs, hooves instead of human feet. The legs were bent at an unnatural angle, closer to a dog's hind legs than a human structure.

Its torso was bare, and looked like a human's stomach.

McKay wasn't sure, but he believed it had two appendages sprouting from its back, much like the membranous wing's bats possessed.

It had a goat's head with two curled horns adorning the top.

It stepped forward and with outstretched hands that finished in thick claws, ripped the man's head off and eagerly lapped at the blood that poured from the base of his neck.

The camera moved and blurred before refocusing.

The three men were stunned with what they saw next.

A thick set of ropes had been wrapped around the beast.

The parishioners were imprisoning this demon.

A knock on the door caused them all to scream.

McKay flipped off the projector and went to the door. Opening it, he saw a frazzled pizza guy standing there.

"Oh, shit. Sorry. Completely forgot," McKay said, fishing for his wallet.

"Sorry it took so long, mister. That'll be $20. That dead person out front really made it tough to get in here."

"Dead person," McKay quizzed, not sure what the guy meant.

"Yeah. Wait? Didn't you see? Someone killed themselves on your guy's front lawn."

McKay handed the pizza box to Bianchi and went to the window, looking out. Sure enough a scene had been taped off, and a sheet covered a body.

"Well fuck. No, we've been focused in here."

He handed the guy two twenties and then shut the door. He didn't need the change and knew the tip would be appreciated.

"I say we eat, take a minute and then watch whatever the

fuck is next," McKay suggested.

"Sounds good. You got any booze?" Grant asked.

"Bottle in the drawer," McKay replied.

While Grant got the bottle and started to slug it back, McKay looked at Bianchi giving him a '*what the fuck*' look.

"This is extraordinary," Bianchi said. "Just stunning. I think I know what will happen next, but I can't believe this is on film."

"I gotta say, I wasn't expecting to come watch freaky demon porn with you two fucks, but the special effects are impressive on this flick," Grant said.

McKay nodded, surprised at how delicious the pepperoni tasted. He was famished, and this cheese and meat slice of dough was hitting the spot perfectly.

THEY FINISHED EATING, Grant and Bianchi used the washroom, and they all got situated, ready to see this film out.

"Ready?"

Both nodded to McKay. He flipped the switch back on and they heard the whirl of the projector.

The screen flickered and twitched before the reel caught and the scene returned to life.

Now, they watched as the creature came into view.

It was struggling and roaring, the sound close to crossing the years and the void.

"Jesus, fuck," Grant said to himself. Bianchi stared at the footage, face blank and expressionless.

They watched as Father approached the creature, and when he was beside it, he turned and spoke. The camera twisted and showed a gathering of people, all pushed in close.

The camera returned to Father, who motioned with his hands. Three men and three women approached, disrobed and knelt before the creature and the man.

Father reached behind the chair the beast was bound on and produced a handsaw.

When McKay and Bianchi saw that, they both turned to look at the two pieces of six-inch horn sitting on the desk. Grant saw them turn, so he followed their heads to see what they were looking at.

"Fuck no. Fuck off. Seriously?" he said, scrambling to his feet. He moved away from the desk but continued watching the footage.

As Father sawed back and forth, first through the end of one horn and then the other, the six people kneeling before the beast were chanting something. Bianchi was trying to read their lips.

"Sheol. That's what they're chanting. They are summoning the underworld," he finally said.

A redheaded woman appeared, McKay recognizing her immediately.

She walked before each of the kneeling people, and slit their throats one at a time.

When the six had fallen, she turned and kneeled before the beast.

Father finished cutting the horns off. One done with that, he reached down to the crotch of the beast and produced its penis.

The woman leaned in and while she began to perform fellatio on the beast, Father stabbed the creature in the chest with a long, sharp object. McKay's hand throbbed. Father started cutting away a section of its left breast.

McKay was transfixed. Watching the woman's head bob

up and down. Watching the beast strain and writhe, trying to break free. Watching the rhythmic way in which Father cut the section of the beast.

When he'd made a jagged circle in its chest, Father pulled the section of tissue away. The man appeared to punch the opening, his hand working deep inside the chest cavity.

"He's pulling out the heart," Bianchi said. McKay knew he was right.

From behind the three men, they heard a sound.

They all turned and looked, finding the source immediately.

"No fucking way," Grant said.

The soft black sack that had been in the wooden box pulsated.

"Are you fucking trying to tell me that a demon's heart is in that sack?"

McKay looked back at the footage.

The woman stood, apparently finished.

Father held something in his hand. He looked euphoric.

He dropped to his knees and took a bite from the dark thing he held.

The beast let out a bellow, its mouth gaping wide, before it slumped and ceased moving.

The three men watched as the woman brought a sack that looked identical to the one on McKay's desk and Father placed the flesh inside.

The camera followed as Father walked to a wide table and placed the two cut pieces of horn as well as the sack inside.

The footage ended as the lid was closed.

"This is a big fucking elaborate joke, yeah? Like, you two assholes called me over here, and now I got to sit through some shitty silent movie as a joke. Right, McKay? Fuck."

The projector was still rattling around as the film had come off the spool and McKay hadn't made the effort to flip the switch. He was struggling to process a few things.

The sack was still pumping and pulsating on the desk. It was as though whatever Father had done on the screen had evoked some power and brought whatever was inside to life. McKay could feel his thighs and hand bleeding. He didn't want to look at the bandage on his palm or the tensor wraps. He knew they'd be soaked through.

He also couldn't explain why he was so aroused, to the point that he was certain if he so much as stood the pressure of his pants against his erection would cause him to ejaculate.

Grant paced the room, becoming more and more animated. Bianchi stood silently. McKay did notice it looked like the man was silently crying, tears cascading over his cheeks.

Just what the fuck had they watched?

McKay flipped the projector off, and waited until he felt safe to stand.

"I need some air," he said, neither men paying mind.

He opened the door and was greeted by an officer about to knock.

"What's up?"

"McKay, we need you outside. The incident is related to your case."

"It is?"

"Yeah, there's a few connections."

He followed the officer, caught off guard. McKay knew he looked like shit, stunk, and was as far away from appearing professional as possible. Hopefully the media presence was minimal outside or he'd get chewed out when the footage aired.

"What do we got?"

The two homicide detectives standing there turned and smirked.

"Fuck, McKay. You need to pay your girls better. That way they won't have their pimps fuck you up." They both burst out laughing but stopped when they saw McKay's face.

"I'm in no fucking mood, and now this shit out here. So, what do we got?"

McKay inspected the body, took a few notes, before following the two back inside.

It was in here that they showed him the security footage of the incident.

As soon as McKay heard the chanting, and saw the figure approach and leave, he understood how this was related.

"Send me the footage, and assign an officer to that body when it's transported."

Heading back to his office, McKay was surprised to detect something in his gut. Almost a yearning, or longing, as though the distance he'd put between himself and the sack had caused some emotional hurt.

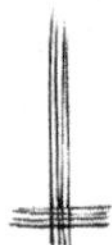

When he returned to his office, Grant had calmed down. He was sitting in his chair, hands behind his head. His armpits had soaked through from sweat, matching McKay's own shirt.

Bianchi was furiously typing away on the laptop.

Surprisingly, the sack still sat on the desk, the material rising and falling.

"You look in this?"

"Fuck no, McKay. I was waiting for you to return so I can sign whatever and get the fuck out of here. I need to go get blackout drunk so I never remember this day."

McKay slid the document to the man, who produced a pen, signed it, and left without saying a word.

"What now?"

Bianchi looked up, running McKay's question around in his brain.

"I hesitate to answer. Only because I don't believe you'll like my reply."

McKay sat, feeling his pants squish as he made contact. It wouldn't feel good when he tried to take them off later.

"Shoot."

"I think we both need some distance from this. I think we both go home, try and get some rest, and reconvene tomorrow. You said before that you were trying to determine a motive for what occurred at the cult complex? I think we've found the why. Father regretted imprisoning or eliminating the presence. The ritual performed was to bring the entity back into the flesh. They wanted to open the black heavens, but I believe Abaddon would only allow that to happen if its heart and horns were returned."

"Fuck's sake. That makes sense."

"Unfortunately, from what I've been reading here on the dark web, that would be the order of things. I suspect, and it's only a hunch, that the redheaded woman from before wanted you to see what happened, but she'll be returning for this box."

McKay knew this already. He'd suspected it from their first encounter.

"When I first met the woman, after she stabbed me, she said to go to Preacher's Rock. I'm going to head out there now. You go home, Bianchi. You've been a great help. I'll see you tomorrow."

Bianchi nodded, folded his laptop, replaced it in his briefcase and shook McKay's hand.

Once he was alone, McKay closed the door and licked his lips. He wanted to look in the pouch, see what was pulsating. But something deep inside told him to wait.

He went to auto and signed out a patrol car.

As McKay drove back to the complex, he felt that pain of distance from the sack and the horns growing once again.

Job 7:8
The eye that beholds me will see me no more;
while your eyes are upon me, I shall be gone.

CHAPTER THIRTY

McKay parked his car and limped through the now abandoned commune. It had been just over a week since the mass suicide had occurred, but with the state this place looked today, it could have happened decades ago.

The blank, dark windows glared at him as he shuffled through the center of the buildings, walked by the entrance to the worship area, and proceeded to follow the path away from the dwellings. Discarded police tape fluttered haphazardly around the area.

Preacher's Rock loomed beyond the complex. It was only a short distance away, but with McKay's current condition and the sweltering heat, he felt like he had been walking for hours when he finally arrived at the base.

He immediately spotted the area from his vision, where Father had impregnated Lily. It made him feel repulsed when he thought back to that moment.

McKay didn't know what he was supposed to look for, but he figured there was a specific reason the woman had suggested he return here.

He searched the clearing where the candles had been placed in the vision, morbidly wondering if any of the impressions on the ground were the place where Lily had lain.

McKay circled the base of the mountainous outcropping. Even in exhaustion and physical hell, his keen eyes darted back and forth. His occupation dictated he looked for the one thing that didn't belong.

It was as he was about to give up looking in this area and make the trek up the path that he caught it. A glint of something metallic reflecting deeper under an overhang.

He stooped down and shuffled to the spot. He wiped the dirt and dust away, letting his eyes fall on what reflected.

It was a marker. A simple metal arrow pointing deeper.

"Well fuck."

He pulled out his cellphone and hit the flashlight app. The overhang was more of a cave, he saw. He moved along slowly, thighs screaming, taking care not to bash his head on the rock roof.

When he made it to what he believed to be the back surface, he saw that it wasn't a rock wall at all. It was a stone slab leaning at an angle.

McKay pulled it and stepped away as it fell to the ground, hitting with a thud, throwing dust everywhere. He knew he'd never be able to lift it on his own, but he didn't care.

He looked at what now stood before him.

An opening.

An entrance to a stairwell that led down.

CHAPTER THIRTY-ONE

His flashlight app lit the way as he followed the stone stairs deeper under the surface.

McKay saw the telltale signs he'd expect to see in a place like this; sconces to hold lit torches, uneven steps, and the ever-growing claustrophobia of darkness above.

He no longer could make out the opening when he looked back, the light from the surface snuffed out.

Another half dozen steps and McKay came to the bottom. A chamber stretched out before him. Twenty feet by twenty feet, the light from his phone showed him that he was alone.

In the middle of the room was a slab with what looked like a sarcophagus on it.

McKay examined the walls first. Much like at a crime scene, he rarely went straight to the victim. He wanted to get an idea of the layout, the surroundings first. Look at where the incident happened before focusing on the main event.

The walls had crude carvings on them. It was hard to

make out what they were supposed to depict, but he did see some Latin and some bible verse numbers.

He didn't spend much time on them, not seeing anything of pertinent importance.

McKay made his way to the middle of the room.

Standing over the sarcophagus, he saw that there were six words etched into the top.

Lily. Ascended to the black heavens.

McKay pushed the lid as hard as he could, the weight double that of the stone slab blocking the entrance to the stairs.

His entire body screamed at him, his thighs and hand the most. Mckay's nose started to bleed from the exertion, but once the lid started to move, he didn't stop, knowing he'd never get it started again.

The lid finally slid far enough over that gravity forced it to tumble and slam to the floor.

Dust exploded out from the exposed inside, the stink of stale air and rot hitting McKay.

Looking inside, he saw why.

CHAPTER THIRTY-TWO

The mummified remains of a woman lay within.

Some sort of preservation techniques had been administered.

She was on her back, holding a skull in her hands. The skull was sitting on her stomach. In the middle of the skull's forehead was a round hole. From what McKay had been shown in the vision, he knew who that skull belonged to.

The woman, remarkably, still had skin on her body. She had a tattered robe draped around her, but most of her torso and chest was exposed. The parts of her legs he could see, were covered in thick scars.

Where the head would have been was the most unsettling.

Sitting atop the corpse was a cow's head. Its tongue had been cut off, leaving the grey mush of the remains to dangle out one side. Its eyes were glassy, somehow still full of fluid. Around its nostrils were red globs, which looked to be dried blood, but without analysis McKay was speculating. This explained the stench of rot. Someone had put this cow's head here recently.

McKay leaned in, looking closely at the necklace around the base of the body's neck. While he peered closer, he heard a soft padding sound from behind him, as though someone was approaching on bare feet.

He stiffened as the air shifted behind him.

McKay could feel breathing hitting his neck. There, gone. There, gone.

Whatever was behind him whispered then; *"Father arise."*

McKay swung around, determined to punch or grab the intruder. Finding he was still alone in the chamber did nothing to settle his nerves.

"Come on! Who's there?"

He shone the light in all directions, still coming up blank.

Seeing nothing, he returned to the corpse. Something about that necklace had caught his attention.

He reached in and delicately lifted it up so that he could see the plate that was attached to the metal loop.

"What the fuck?"

The plate read McKay.

Out of the corner of his eye he caught a subtle twitch, a movement barely perceptible.

He straightened and looked at the cow's head.

Then it blinked.

CHAPTER THIRTY-THREE

The drive back to the precinct was as much of a blur for McKay as the pained sprint from the chamber to the car.

Somehow, he ended up sitting at his desk.

All the while he had flashes of the cow's head blinking, of the whispered voice from behind him as he hustled up the stairs, and the blare of car horns as he weaved in and out of traffic.

By nightfall he was spent.

He wanted to return home, but felt safer and more grounded in the real world by remaining at the station.

While he decided on what he needed to do, he buzzed the desk of an officer working late in the work space.

Officer White hurried to McKay's office.

"You rang, McKay?"

"You were a medic in the army, right?"

"I was. Why's that?"

"I need some help, off the record. Are you willing to help with some bandages, but no report?"

"$100."

"Deal. Come in, close the door and shut the blinds please."

White did as asked, and sat on the chair.

"So, where we working on?"

"My hand and my thighs."

White's eyebrows went up.

"I heard about the crazy who stabbed your hand. It was a nail, yeah?"

White's words caused his head to spin. The room tumbled and twirled, his stomach lurching.

"Jesus, here," White said, handing the waste basket to McKay. The timing was perfect as McKay vomited into the basket.

He had been stabbed through the hand with a nail. Father had stabbed Abaddon with a long, sharp object. Most likely a nail. Lily had been lobotomized with a nail. More bile rose. He knew full well that he could never prove it, but he was positive it would be the same nail.

"Sorry," McKay mumbled, not wanting to reveal what was actually making him ill. "Haven't ate much. Blood loss as well. Just dizzy."

"Sure. You're the boss. I'm not going to argue with $100."

McKay showed him his bled-through bandage on his hand, before he stood and dropped his pants revealing the glistening red tensor bandages. A smell permeated the air.

"Fuck man. When did that happen? That smells infected."

"I think it was last night? Two nights ago? I can't actually remember. I've been burning the candle at both ends here with this case."

"Let me get some supplies. Just sit here," White said.

He returned a short time later with a fully stocked first-aid kit.

"Look, I'll clean you up and make it as pretty as I can, but you need to get some antibiotics. Infections are not something to fuck around with."

McKay nodded, and started to remove his tensor wraps.

"Fuck me," he grimaced, pain shooting up his legs as the stuck part of the tensor pulled away from his wounds.

White went to work, dabbing, wiping and dabbing some more. When all was said and done, McKay's thighs and hand were rebandaged and for a brief second the throbbing disappeared.

"Thank you."

"Any time. Now pay up," he chuckled.

McKay grabbed his wallet and handed the man two fifties.

"You need a lift home?" White asked, pocketing the cash.

"Nah. I'm going to finish some notes and I'll get a lift from someone later."

White said his goodbyes and left McKay alone.

McKay stared at the scattered debris on his desk.

It was odd. Now that he'd returned and the distance between him and the sack was so small, his pain was less.

He picked up the sack and moved his hand with the mass inside as it expanded and contracted.

Placing the sack back in the wooden box, he retrieved the two pieces of horn and put them in as well. He placed the photos into the envelope and tucked that in as well. Finally, he closed the lid and put the box back into the stone container.

McKay wiped his brow, put the stone lid back on top, before picking it up and leaving his office. He closed and locked the door behind him, before he crossed the work floor.

Dread and guilt filled him as he tried not to bring any attention to himself.

He got to the front desk, made brief small talk with the night desk clerk, then stepped outside.

The rain had stopped hours ago, but the air was damp and heavy.

Instead of getting patrol to drop him off, he decided to hail a cab.

The ride home was short.

McKay entered his house tentatively, expecting to be ambushed by the redhead.

Instead he found his home as he'd left it.

His bedroom was still in a state of disarray.

Blankets scattered, and clothes strewn about.

The weight of everything slammed down on him.

McKay set the stone box beside his bed and changed from his suit. It felt good to put on some shorts and a t-shirt after so many days of work wear.

Sitting on the bed, his thoughts drifted back to the footage, as well as what he'd seen under Preacher's Rock.

The head had blinked. His name had been on that necklace.

None of it made sense.

He felt his hand throb again, as though thinking of that hole in the skull had created a connection with his injury.

McKay couldn't fight sleep anymore.

Too many long days and longer nights.

The visit, the footage, the photos, the trip to Preacher's Rock.

It all caught up to him as sleep take over his brain.

He pulled the sheet back, content to use it as his blanket, and crawled onto the bed and experienced a release of stress as his head gently connected with his pillow. His nose reminded him to limit the pressure, so he adjusted his position and let out a long breath.

McKay was snoring within seconds.

As the man began to snore, the woman stepped from the shadows.

She walked silently, stopping alongside McKay.

She caressed his face, feeling guilt over the damage she'd inflicted. Physically and mentally.

McKay was nothing but a vessel for them. A man at the wrong place at the wrong time, forced into these events by his job. Unfortunately for him, the ritual of Abaddon called for the sacrifice of an educated innocent. McKay now fit that bill.

Retrieving her stone box, she opened the lid, removed the sack, and opened the top. She took the mass out, looking at the ancient heart with a chunk of flesh missing.

"Father arise."

The wall rippled and darkened, before Father stepped through.

He was wearing a robe, the front stained red.

McKay rustled and turned, hearing the sounds behind

him. Seeing the woman and Father, he scurried to the head of his bed, legs pulled up tight.

"The fuck? Your burned body was at the scene of that massacre," McKay said, embarrassed with the screech in his voice.

"My earthly body maybe. An immortal never dies."

The woman handed something to Father, McKay unable to see.

The old man stepped towards McKay, staring unnervingly at the detective.

"None of this makes sense. You're responsible for the deaths of your flock. I'll need you to put your hands behind your back," McKay said, feeling emboldened with the familiarity of his job.

"My son. There is nothing left for you here. You've played your role. You've helped us connect the cosmic dots we needed connected. Sleep now."

McKay went to reply, to try and de-escalate the situation, but before he could begin, Father lashed out, his arm moving faster than McKay believed an old man could.

A shriek left his mouth as the nail went through his skin, his skull and lodged into his brain.

A series of grunts followed, his tongue lolled and saliva began to leak profusely.

The last cognizant thought he had was *stop*, as he watched Father and the redhead walk through the black, before it returned to wall.

CHAPTER THIRTY-FIVE

Bianchi had waited outside McKay's locked office for two hours before he finally got a ride over to his house.

He pounded on the door for some time, before deciding he'd had enough.

He heard a noise from inside, a snort or a huff, and after what he'd seen on that footage, he wasn't about to just leave.

Bianchi kicked the door twice before it gave up and burst inwards.

Entering, he came to an immediate stop when he spotted McKay.

The detective was shuffling around his living room.

His mouth was open, his eyes wide, and he was moaning without interruption. Bianchi could see the drool that coated his chin.

McKay was wearing a t-shirt and shorts and when the man circled around, Bianchi could see that McKay had pissed and shit himself several times over.

At first Bianchi believed that McKay's nose had busted open again and was bleeding, but when he focused on his face, Bianchi saw that it was because of the nail that protruded from the middle of his forehead.

"Fuck," he said once. He stepped outside and called 911, knowing that his lifelong search of proving Abaddon was a real, physical entity had encountered another roadblock.

When the photo of himself sitting with Brad and the girl had been found in the envelope, he'd held his breath. He didn't believe McKay would've recognized him when he was so young, but he still had been alarmed.

He hit a speed dial number on his phone and waited while it rang.

"Hello." The voice said when they answered.

"McKay's role is complete. I've seen proof. The box has vanished. I'll see you in France."

He hung up. When the sirens approached, he sat and watched the sky darken.

It was times like these Bianchi wished he smoked.

END

I was petrified when I released Ritual.

I absolutely loved the story, and Father is a unique char-acter. It also let me run through some demonology stuff that I've wanted to touch on. But it is a very stark turn from my other releases. Don't get me wrong – if you've read my stuff, you'll know damn well that I like to go dark and awful – but Ritual went to another level. Graphic, sadistic, and in some places gratuitous – all to tell this horrible story. I was surprised at the response. I really was. I want to believe it was because the price point was awesome ($0.99 for the ebook) and the cover is DA BOMB. But, shockingly, people really seemed to connect with the depravity of the story. Beyond surprising was seeing it listed on the recommended reading list for the Stoker's. I never once believed it would carry on further, but what a boost.

Secondly – when I finished Ritual, I barfed out a sequel and a very rough trilogy finale. I've refined the sequel several times now, then waited to see if people would want to read more. It was one particular review that cemented that the demand to see more was there (no, not the 1-star review, which has been a godsend for interest FYI! As of writing this Ritual has six 1-star reviews). It was from my friend Diamond. Her review actually touched on a bit of the direction I'd went with the sequel, and seeing that cosmic connection on Goodreads – all systems were go.

So, as you saw, book two is dedicated to DIE!mond. Thank you for your kind words, but also never sugar coating anything. It's meant a ton!

With Ritual, I did two key bits – Bible Verses and a poem. For this one, I canned the poem part. I felt if I did it again, it would feel like I was reaching to just rehash Ritual. I messaged a few folks and they all said they could live with or without it. Good enough.

As for the Bible Verses. I think they are paramount for two reasons.

The first is that the story within COMMUNION is really based on a rabid, blind faith. Much like the devout can utilize the vagueness of the bible, Father can use his visions and the documents he has to try and open the black heavens. More so though, is McKay and Bianchi's search for answers – no matter the cost.

The bible verses chosen here all relate to Abaddon and Sheol in one form or another. Abaddon and Sheol are co-linked throughout numerous versions of the bible, both as entities/figures as well as places. From the research I've done, neither was ever considered a 'demon' per se, but that's pretty close to the role I've put them in here.

The second reason I chose to use the bible verse structure again is connectivity. While I didn't want to rehash anything directly from Ritual, I did want the trilogy to have a flow and a similar feeling.

Book three will finish the trilogy off, and if you can gather – Bianchi will be in hot pursuit. It will pick up in France and from what I have outlined, I think it's a worthy conclusion to a repulsive character.

I don't want to give anything away here, but if time is on my side, I may be able to get book three out this year (2020) as well. We'll see. I have the bare bones done, but need to flesh it out.

So, thanks so much to all you folks reading this, glad you've come along for the ride.

Most of the time I thank a bunch of folks individually here, but for this one – thank you to everyone out there, you all rock.

Until we meet again.

Steve

SACRAMENT
Steve Stred

the battle
raged
on and on...

1:1
**"Before there was light, before there was dark,
there was only chaos"**

BETWEEN

"I stand before you, your Father, the *chosen*. I stand as the true vision of chaos and energy, of cosmic connection and hope. Come my children, return to our land."

Father stepped aside, as the flock ascended from the darkened passageway that travelled under Preacher's Rock and made their way to the commune hidden on the northern side of the land mass. The Lords from above had long ago prepared the areas around the portal that existed through Preacher's Rock. To dig back the layers of sand in the miles that surrounded the area would reveal the remains of previous colonies, of prior failures from those determined to be unholy and not worthy of ascension.

Father grinned, saliva pooling around his rotting teeth. His eyes darted from member to member, looking at the collection of new parishioners she'd gathered for him. He watched her mingle among the recruits, smiling, welcoming. She reminded Father of her mother so much, it made his groin ache. He chastised himself for those thoughts. He still saw himself as a holy man, one above such disgusting and sinful desires.

He took some tentative steps forward, leaning heavily on his crudely fashioned crutches. His hoofed feet shuffled along the dirt, his thighs concealed behind his robe, but the pain that coursed through his legs where they'd been attached brought the threat of him passing out.

They'd been questioning where their Father had been, where the leader was for the past few days as he'd undergone the procedure. They didn't need to worry about what he was going through. He did this all for ascension. For himself. He did it for them as well, so they'd know true pain and sacrifice would be needed.

Soon, he thought. *Soon, the pain will leave. I have made myself in my Lord's image. Once the flock follows suit, only then will the Black Heavens finally allow entry.*

Arriving at the bench he'd had placed beside his hut, he sat, resting an arm on the stone box. The box that contained Abbadon's horn.

Professor Bianchi remained and answered every question the police asked, followed by more questions from two detectives.

McKay had been transported from the house some time earlier, loaded onto a gurney and into an ambulance. He never looked at Bianchi. He had continued walking in circles, moaning and groaning in the house while Bianchi remained on the steps. The poor man was drooling profusely even as the doors of the ambulance closed, eyes staring into the distance.

Bianchi had a pain in his heart he hadn't expected. He'd developed a fondness for the man, however brief their time together was.

"Free to go, Professor," the taller detective said, flipping his notepad closed.

He gave them a nod and climbed into the cab they had kindly called for him.

Before the car pulled away, there was a rap on the window.

He lowered the window and looked up at the detective.

"One last thing. We may have some follow ups, so don't stray too far."

"I don't plan on," he replied with a smile.

He stared out the window for the entire drive to the airport. Nobody batted an eyelid at him as he checked in and boarded the plane.

Bianchi fell asleep shortly after liftoff, and only awoke after touchdown when the stewardess gently shook his arm to let him know they'd landed.

"Thank you," he replied, grabbing his briefcase.

It wasn't until he hailed a cab and they started to leave Paris that a heavy weight began to develop in his stomach.

It had been far too long since he'd visited his parents' house.

Now, it was a six hour cab ride south west and he'd be home.

Outside, it started to rain.

The driveway up to his parents' manor was a single car width. It was comprised of packed dirt, so unused that weeds and grass grew abundantly down the middle between the tire tracks.

Bianchi wished he could see the driver's face when they left the tree-enclosed driveway and exited into the large cement area before the large house, hidden far off the main road.

He handed the driver a wad of cash and asked him to wait. Bianchi didn't believe he'd be here long, but he didn't want the hassle of having to wait for another cab.

He left the car, using his briefcase to shield himself from the rain, and jogged up the three levels of concrete steps that led to the double wood doors.

The doors were open when he arrived, a short man standing waiting.

"Professor, welcome. Your father is in the dining room."

He gave the man a nod, stepping around and leaving him

to close the doors. Bianchi kept his briefcase with him, wanting to make sure he knew where his possessions were.

He walked down the long hallway that ran directly through the middle of the house. His dad had used that to break up the functionality of the rooms. On the left were the living areas, on the right the business areas.

Arriving at the dining room, Bianchi walked in, not bothering to announce his arrival.

He saw the man sitting at the end of the table. The table had already been cleared, a glass near an outstretched hand the only remaining item.

"Hello, Father," Bianchi said.

"Don't you EVER fucking call me that!" the man replied, slamming his fists to the table top. The glass toppled, the fluid within splashing across the floor.

Bianchi looked to the man's face, seeing the rage in his eyes. His lips were pursed, cheeks puffed out with anger. Little flecks of spittle bubbled at the corner of his mouth.

"I'm sorry. *Dad*. That better?"

"Sit, you ungrateful fuck," the man replied, face remaining red.

"I'll stand, if it's all the same," Bianchi said.

"Fine, whatever. What news brings you all this way, so that we are graced with your presence?"

"Father has the box."

The man's eyes darted around, the news clattering throughout his brain.

"They've made great progress. An innocent was invaded. I was able to see photographs and watch video taken of the Lord stepping through the void, into our world."

At those words the man's eyes snapped to Bianchi's, a glow lit deep within.

"Here?"

Bianchi nodded. He set his briefcase on the table, popped the locks, and retrieved some of the photos he'd managed to take from McKay's office as well as some he'd printed out. The old man leaned close, looking at the evidence. His hands shook as he greedily licked his lips. Bianchi wasn't about to let him take ownership of the situation. He grabbed the photos and stuffed them back into the case, clipping and closing the lid.

The man popped the brakes from his wheelchair and moved away from the table, rolling around to face Bianchi.

Bianchi couldn't bring himself to look at the man's atrophied thighs, the lifeless dangling hoofs that didn't reach the foot rests.

"What does this mean?"

"It means we're running out of time," Bianchi replied. "It means Father will do unto others as he's done unto you. He'll try and make the flock in *its* image. And if he succeeds in doing that, I believe the gates will finally open and ascendency will be achieved."

"Immortality?"

"Cosmic immortality."

"You must go. Go to Preacher's Rock. Go below, as above. Find the entrance to where Father has them now, and stop them. We both know if that gate is opened, chaos will rain down from the stars."

Bianchi nodded, grabbed his briefcase and began walking away from the long table.

"Son?"

He stopped, not turning. It'd been many decades since he'd been called that.

CHAPTER 2

"Before you go, you must visit your mother. It may be the last time you can."

Bianchi left the dining room, knowing he'd not prepared himself to see her.

CHAPTER 3

The door groaned on its hinges as he pushed it open.

The room was pitch black, the window boarded over some time ago.

A stench grabbed him by his neck, wringing bile up from the pit of his stomach. It was the mixture of rotting flesh, pus, piss, and shit that only this room could smell of. He didn't believe it had ever smelled different.

"Mother?"

A weak groan sounded from ahead, an attempt to call him to the bed.

He didn't want to walk into the room, but knew he had to. Something squished under his foot as he took a step closer. His eyes adjusted to the gloom, the outline of the bed and her body started to reveal itself.

The flicker of a candle coming to life illuminated the room, the wax having burned itself down to the point that it flowed over the metal dish below the base, the flame dancing from the wick.

Bianchi couldn't believe the state of her.

A brown and red stain bloomed around her rail-thin body, the vastness of the formerly white sheet making her look even more miniscule.

"Mom..." he heard himself whisper, his voice low. Something told him to not speak too loudly, for fear of waking unseen things in the darkened corners.

She lay exposed on the bed, naked and weathered. Her one human leg had wasted away, now pushed awkwardly under her animal appendage. The two pronged hoof shifted subtly, his breath inhaling sharply at the motion.

The wrinkles and folds of her abdomen weren't enough to hide the jagged scar that went from hip to hip, the glaring reminder of the child Father had cut forth from her in one of his failed ritual attempts.

Her formerly large breasts were now hanging over her ribs, the deflated fatty sacs of flesh and nipple resting in the crook of her elbows. Her arms bent slightly so that the dried corpse of a fetus was cradled in her hands.

The love of a mother knew no bounds.

Another groan, Bianchi's eyes finding hers, surprised that she had the strength to even lift her eyelids enough to see.

"Mom, I'm sorry I've been away," he said, keeping his voice as quiet as possible. "I'm sorry this is your life. I'll do my best, and I promise you, if that gate is opened, I will find a way to take this pain from you and get you through to the Black Heavens."

He tried but failed to let his gaze drift over the rest of her head. He knew what he'd find there; the nail protruding from the middle of her forehead, the long hair cut short, the festering sores from where she lay.

Something shifted in the blackness of the room. A deep rumble from the depths of a creature's belly sounded, followed by the forced exhalation of air. That was his signal to retreat.

Bianchi fled the room, the short man waiting outside to close and barricade the door behind him. He walked at a pace nearing a jog, down the hallway, out the door and through the torrential rain to the waiting cab.

"Where to?" the driver asked once his door was closed.

"Airport."

The cab pulled away from the mansion hidden in the forests of France. As it did, Bianchi looked back, seeing the silhouette of a beast in the large window that overlooked the courtyard.

2:9
From hoof and horn the flock will be summoned,
gathered to dance and rejoice

The agonizing yells of pain coming from Father's tent were drowned out by the congregations singing as they went about their daily routines.

Men came and went along the outside perimeter, fortifying the meagre fencing that had been erected decades before.

Within the confines of the encampment, the women sang loudly while picking food from the gardens or washing clothes.

All around, the children they'd brought played and caroused, unaware of the howls of suffering that came and went from the leader's living space.

Morning made way for afternoon as the sun travelled over the parishioners below, Father's screams coming closer and closer together.

As afternoon became night, a group of worried followers gathered around the entrance to the canvas tent, watching with concern as pail after pail of blood was removed from inside.

When the rest of the members assembled around the growing bonfire to dance and sing, the redheaded woman stepped forth and addressed those still standing at the entrance.

"Fear not. Our Father has made yet another momentous step towards ascendancy. His transformation continues, and as long as our Lord wills it, you'll see his new form tomorrow."

She smiled, before disappearing back into the tent. Those close enough were able to catch a glimpse of the scene within, of dark things huddled over the frail man, of patches of blood trailing across the floor, and of a shadow over the bed that showed how dedicated Father truly was for the cause.

CHAPTER 5

"Come! Come one and all, and rejoice! Our Father has returned from his communion with the cosmic gods, spoken with Belial and Abaddon and Sheol! Chaos has infused his soul! Come, and see true transcendency before your very eyes!"

The redheaded woman called out as she walked through the sleeping areas, waking the people as she went. To a man, her name was unknown. Through the teachings they had come to know she was the daughter of Lily and Father, but her name had been kept from their lips. For why? This was not a lesson they'd been taught yet.

But her word was Law, and as she bellowed at them, they made their way to the rocky area that served as one of the numerous pulpits for Father to deliver his sermons.

The group stood, scattered around the area with no semblance of order. The burned remains of the fires from the previous night created space between the gathered parishioners, the wind picking up as they waited.

A murmur began, sweeping across the members as more

and more joined in. At first, those standing furthest back were not privy to what the unrest was about, but as the people began kneeling from the front and it travelled back in a wave, they gasped and kneeled before the living embodiment of chaos.

Before Father.

The old man hobbled forth, his hoofed feet scuffing the dirt, his fur-covered legs now strong enough to support his thin upper body. He still used a cane to walk, needing it for balance. His white robe was caked in filth, stains of red running across it.

But it wasn't the arrival of Father that had signalled them to kneel. It was the thick horns that curled from his forehead, one on either side. The Gods had granted him inclusion. Abaddon had deemed Father worthy to take the final shape and move within a single step of the ritual to open the Black Heavens and allow the gathered to ascend for true cosmic chaos immortality.

Before he stepped behind the pulpit, he held his frail arms out to the sides, the redhead stepping in for an embrace. Once done, she stepped back, and he turned to face his congregation.

Still kneeling, each member felt the cold grip of death flow through them as he met them with a sneer on his face.

"And to think... some of you *doubted* me!"

He stepped back, taking them all in, looking at each and every face. It was as though Father was looking for a denier to step forth, to speak what some had only whispered behind closed doors.

"WELL?"

He spat a thick gob of blood to the ground, licking his lips. Still all stayed low and silent.

"Here we are. Together. While out there," he waved his hands rapidly around, "the battle rages on and on. Hatred towards us. Hatred towards what we cherish and wish to achieve. To them, to them I say this. BOW BEFORE ME! A dark God from the cosmos in the flesh!"

Father punctuated the ending with a flourish as his hands whipped around in the air. The sneer never left his face as he left the roost he'd been preaching from. The redhead helped him back to his tent, leaving the congregation wide eyed and open mouthed. What they'd witnessed ignited the fuel within for ascendency.

No one noticed Bianchi standing off to the side, taking in the spectacle. He would never have believed that what Father had done to himself was possible. But having seen it now, with his own eyes, he knew he needed to find Abaddon's Box and stop the man from opening the Black Heavens.

Father kept one eye on the group as they dispersed. His main attention was fixed on the man in the black suit standing apart from the rest. He recognized the professor immediately, even if it had been years since he'd been plucked from their group and fled with his parents. Thinking of Bianchi's mother, and how she had failed to deliver that child to him, to the group, made him seethe with rage.

She had one job.

Now she remained in the clutches of dark energy, not fully in this realm or the next.

He turned to shuffle to the bed, the right horn catching on the opening of the tent, the canvas a heavy enough material to provide some resistance. He howled in agony as the base of the horn squelched as it shifted against his forehead. He fell to the bed, rapidly breathing, the shooting flames of hurt flaring up in his temples. Blood leaked from the poorly done stitches that circled the base.

"Father, are you OK?"

He didn't know who asked. It was a female voice, one of

the numerous servants he'd given himself to ensure he was pampered.

He grunted a response, the throbbing not diminishing on the side of his head.

A light breeze crossed over him, someone entering into the tent. He smelled her before she was beside him, his daughter kneeling and taking his hand.

"Father, Bianchi is here. I spotted him as you left your sermon."

"I know," he replied, each word a struggle to say.

"Should we be concerned?"

"Yes, my dear. Find him and tell him I request a meeting. I know he wishes for our failure. But more than anything, he wishes for our grasp on his mother to relinquish, for her to not be held hostage any longer."

She nodded. Turning, she saw the lone servant girl and smiled. She motioned with her head once before pushing through the tent flap and leaving them alone.

"Not today," Father said, knowing the young woman was reaching for his cock. "The holy fluids are primed for procreation, and we can't have that. You there," he said, towards the man washing bloody towels in a basin.

"You, come. Relieve me of my tension."

Bianchi walked away from the commune as fast as he could once he realized Hekate had spotted him. Her red hair worked as a beacon. He'd hoped she wouldn't have seen him, but he found himself transfixed by her. Her ascendency had also begun.

Flames a dozen feet high spiralled from her hair, and her eyes burned into him as she watched. The congregation was unable to see any of this, but he knew they would feel the heat from her inferno when they were near.

He could see Preacher's Rock looming in the distance, a perpetual reminder of his current situation. Bianchi wouldn't feel safe until he'd made his way back through the catacombs below and saw the sun on the other side.

"Stop, Professor."

Her call brought him to a halt like a shotgun blast.

"Imagine my surprise seeing you mingling with *our* people," she said, voice noticeably closer.

He forced himself to turn, finding her twenty feet away.

From here the flames looked to be serpents dancing above her head, their own auras glowing orange to red.

"Imagine my surprise finding an old man with horns and hoofs."

She smirked, knowing full well Bianchi was the most knowledgeable of everyone but Father of the steps necessary for the Black Heavens to open.

"Don't play dumb. We always suspected you'd return to the flock, at least to satiate your academic mind."

"We are not family, so do not pretend. What your... *Father* did to my parents is unforgivable."

She laughed out loud at this, as though he'd just told her the world's most hilarious joke in a crowded bar. He felt rage bubble up from deep within, but forced himself to squash it. This was what she wanted, after all. For him to do something irrational and give her a reason to unleash her fury.

"Bianchi, calm yourself. No need to get so worked up. I've not come to harm you. Father has sent me to offer an invitation. He'd like to have a word. He wants to come to some sort of truce, maybe even for the benefit of your parents."

"What? Is he magically going to return my dad's legs? Bring mom back to life instead of being a trapped soul in a rotting body?"

She smiled, which filled Bianchi with a dread he didn't know was possible to feel. Something far behind those teeth and her eyes answered his questions.

Against his better judgement he started walking after her when she turned, heading towards a meeting with Father.

They didn't speak as she led him back towards where Father's parishioners lived. He kept some distance between them, keeping his eyes off her figure. When they were kids she'd often make him uncomfortable by sitting on his lap and wiggling or pushing her budding chest against him. Now, with Father's transformation and her burgeoning changes, he was cautious that she'd put him under her spell, much like she'd done to McKay.

She had the power, and he was but a pawn.

Father had his end game, the pieces falling into place. Now, they would do whatever it took to ensure their success.

That was what Bianchi hoped to exploit one way or the other. Father knew exactly what Bianchi longed for, what he wished to happen to his own parents. Bianchi knew Father knew this. He'd need to find a way to manipulate the vermin and let his hold on his mom go.

"You know, Father would gladly have you by his side to help us ascend," she said when they arrived at the perimeter fencing.

He looked at the group working, at the dirty clothes, the bodies showing signs of starvation. All for what? The lies the man told them? The hope of immortality? He set his gaze to her eyes, even with the fear her stare drove into him.

"I don't believe I would ever join you. Where is he?"

She kept her eyes on his for so long it became uncomfortable, before she motioned for him to follow.

At the tent, she told him to wait, before disappearing inside. It made him nervous to have her out of his sight, but he didn't expect her to suddenly appear with a gun and shoot him. If anything, he would need to watch for a sleight of hand, and a nail to the frontal lobe.

From within the tent he heard raised voices. Suddenly the tent opened and a man left. Bianchi watched as he walked away, then turned when he heard the clearing of someone's throat.

She stood there, holding one of the flaps open.

"He's waiting," she said, letting Bianchi step in out of the ever-warming sun.

The thing that was Father sat perched on a throne in the back of the tent. Bianchi found it was a larger space than expected, at least from initial outside appearances.

He was slumped back as though he'd been propped into place moments before Bianchi had entered. His animal legs were splayed out, his disgusting robe open and spread out on either side. His flaccid cock hung obscenely between his legs, a sticky fluid seeping from the opening on its head. When Father shifted, a long, thin string of the liquid appeared, keeping the old man's dick still technically in contact with the seat.

Bianchi was repulsed enough seeing that, but when he

fully took in the view of Father's festering, horned head, he gagged and had to cover his mouth to prevent puking.

"You don't seem pleased with my new form?"

"I can smell the rot from here," he replied, watching as Father struggled to sit up straight. "Gangrene already set in?"

The old man rolled his eyes, before he spat a thick wad of phlegm and blood towards Bianchi.

"Such hostility for someone those people outside believe will help them live forever," said Bianchi. "You are Father, after all."

"Bah. They know most won't achieve inclusion. Those whores with children, and those males who fornicate as though rabbits in a field. Sinners, the lot."

"But, the man who leads them is allowed to have men blow him or sit on his dick, as long as *Father* has deemed that necessary?"

"You always were a *different* sort, weren't you? I remember talking with your own father about sacrificing you to Sheol. Our dark Lord wanted to taste the flesh of a toddler, to wrap the skin around its own claws and feel the world as only an infant can. But he didn't have the balls to do it. Look at him now," he said, spitting once again. "How's his attempt to usurp me gone? To make a secret deal with Belial? A man in his position should know there's only one true conduit."

If Bianchi were a larger man, he'd have sprinted forward and pummelled Father until the old man was dead. Instead, he remained silent, wanting to let Father talk himself into a corner.

"You think you're so smart, eh? That's it. Believe you'll let me say or do something that would discredit me or have me fall from grace? You don't know how far my reach is, do you?"

Father let out a loud whistle, a woman appearing in the tent. He snapped his finger and she left. A moment later, she returned, this time with a man of about forty following along.

"Kneel," Father commanded, to which the man dropped to the ground in position.

"Open thy mouth."

The man did as directed, Bianchi watching as the woman helped Father into a standing position.

Bianchi had no interest in watching Father use this man for any purpose. As he turned to leave, Father spoke.

"You leave, you die."

Against his better judgement, he turned back, only to see Father standing before the man with a knife in hand. Before he could say anything, Father brought the knife across the man's throat. As the blood spurted from the wound, he held a golden cup beneath the flow. Once filled, he brought it to his face and poured it over his mouth, drinking some while letting the rest splash over his chin and depressed chest.

The man slumped to the ground, Bianchi watching his descent. He met Father's eyes, a dark pair that blazed with fury.

"I can do no wrong," Father said, in a voice deeper than normal. "Go, before I decide you join him. We'll speak more tomorrow."

Bianchi left without hesitation, knowing his task to stop the leader would be harder than he ever imagined.

9:2
**To dine with the neighbor is to share and shed
blood with true friends**

CHAPTER 9

The butler brought the soup to the table, setting it down before Bianchi's father.

"Thank you. Please, won't you join me?"

"Apologies, sir. I have to finish up with preparations for dinner."

"Very well," Mr. Bianchi replied.

He waited until the man had left the dining room before dipping his spoon into the bowl and bringing the steaming hot fluid to his lips. He gave a gentle blow to try to cool it before sipping.

Sitting back, he shifted in his chair, looking at the far side of the table, at the empty place his wife used to occupy.

Finding himself growing sentimental, he forced the thoughts from entering his head. He had no time for tears or emotions. His son was their last hope, *her* last hope.

A noise from the back corner, deep in the dark shadows, caught his attention. He was about to ignore the shape of the creature that would be lurking there, monitoring him, before it stepped forth into the light.

He gasped, dropping his spoon into the bowl.

Anger flared, his lips trembling, trying to decide whether to yell out or scream.

"Hello, Adam," Father said as he shuffled towards the man.

"You..." was all he could muster in response.

"You sent your weak son to meddle?"

It was then that Adam saw Father's hoofs and what now adorned his head.

"Fuck me... you've actually done it, haven't you," he said, reaching longingly towards the horns.

"I have, old friend."

He knelt in front of the chair, letting him wrap his frail fingers around the thickness of each appendage, bowing his head slightly as he softly stroked up and down the length of each horn.

"I always doubted you," he said softly.

"I know you did. So did she," Father replied, caressing the man's face. "Our watchers ensured she remained viable. For all intents and purposes, she is dead. As are you, Adam."

Adam gave a sheepish smile, as though he was embarrassed at what Father had revealed.

"Abaddon has elevated me, I am no longer a mortal, but a cosmic god. I will join Brad, who became Belial, in the Black Heavens. Sheol has granted it so. Through the underworld I rode, on a black stead made of fire and death. I emerged triumphant, fueled by hatred and filled with venom. Mankind is but an afterthought. Soon, the ascension will occur. You will not be coming. Nor will she. Your son? I can't say. If he does, know that it was his choice. For now, I am here to leave a remnant of sorts. A time capsule, of the potential for future generations to discover my vitality and unlock the cosmic chaos secrets. One last time, I'll deposit my seed. Your son may never learn the truth of who his real father is. But who knows for sure. He's a smart kid, eh? He just may figure it out."

Father walked behind Adam, who was now weeping. He unlocked the brakes of the chair before pulling him out from where he had been stationed. He pushed him out of the dining room, down the hallway, before directing him into his former bedroom.

The stench hit them immediately. It had been some time since he'd visited his wife, letting the demons and the butler tend to her needs. He retched, vomiting what little soup he'd ingested into a darkened area of the room.

"What a reunion!" Father shouted as he twirled around Adam, his robe spinning like a dancer's long dress.

"I remember the old days. Of fucking and philosophising. Of talking long into the night about how we would one day achieve immortality and unlock the secrets of the stars. We've done it, Adam. I'm just so sorry you'll not be joining me."

Father pushed the chair over, throwing Adam to the floor. He walked to the bed and picked up the woman, smiling at her cold face. He kissed her once, then threw her body into the dark corner, the sounds of gleeful disembowelment beginning at once.

"You son of a bitch," Adam began, before Father was on him, ripping off his pants.

"You knew what you signed up for years ago."

His useless legs were no protection, and were unable to help with any escape. Instead, Father pushed him to the floor facedown, over a pillow. The entry wasn't gentle, inner walls ripping as the cockhead forced its way into Adam's ass. As Father pounded away, his balls slapping against Adam's atrophied limbs, his dick began to expand painfully.

"I've missed this," Father said hoarsely into his ear between each thrust.

A warm sensation travelled across Adam's neck. He felt the blood begin to pour, the knife Father had used thrown onto the rug.

"Die as I come," Father bellowed. The creatures in the corner worked into a fervor over the scene before them as they ate.

Long after Adam was dead, Father finally withdrew his shrivelled dick, happy in the knowledge that he'd never need to use it again.

"He's all yours," he said to the shapes in the shadows.

He retrieved his knife before stepping into the darkness and returning to the commune.

The unexpected pattering of rain on the tent's canvas roof woke Bianchi the following morning.

He was disoriented at first, trying to figure out where he was, before it came back.

The commune.

Father.

He groaned as he got to his feet, the reality of sleeping on the ground with only a thin straw mat between him and the dirt hitting his back quickly. A spine used to a memory foam topped mattress hadn't fared well with the change.

The thrumming of the rain hitting the roof picked up, to the point that Bianchi could see it creating small craters near the edge of the canvass walls along the dirt.

Something was off.

He squinted, and stepped towards the edge, his brain trying to process *why* it didn't make sense.

From within the rhythmic tapping of the drops, a symphonic humming began to make its way to Bianchi. He realized it was the sound of numerous humans chanting together.

Throwing open the flaps of the tent, he stared in disbelief at the scene.

The sky was raining blood.

The congregation danced naked below the ichor that fell.

They chanted and swirled, the redness covering every part of their bodies.

For reasons unknown, Bianchi found himself moving forward. He removed his suit jacket, tossing it to the dirt. His fingers fumbled with the buttons of his dress shirt, the sticky fluid making it difficult to slip the little circle through the slot. His belt came next, easily undone and pulled through the loops. He kicked off his leather shoes, his socks following even before the shoes had hit the ground. A middle-aged woman came to him, unbuttoning his pants while kissing him passionately.

Pulling himself away from her coated lips, she took his pants and threw them into a fire burning nearby. As each drop of blood fell and splashed into the flames, a scream sounded that mixed into the gathered choir.

Two men came beside him, stripping his boxers off. At first the feeling of blood spattering onto his suddenly free dick was off putting, but as the dark rain increased in intensity, he felt it stiffen. Only then did he notice every other male was dancing erect.

"I'm glad you've decided to join us," Father said from behind him.

Bianchi whirled around to face the living embodiment of chaos, only to see Hekate standing in his place. Seeing her nude body flooded his brain. He remembered McKay telling him about how she forced herself on his face, and the vision he experienced after.

"How? I heard..."

"You heard me speak through her," Father said, as her mouth moved.

Her hand reached out, pulling him close enough that her nipples touched his chest.

"Bianchi, have you joined us? Turn your head to the sky and open thy mouth. Drink deep of the nectar from our Lords. Only then will you see what is to come."

Hekate pushed her body against his, grinding his cock between their bodies. He looked her in the eyes, before opening his mouth and tilting his head back.

As the blood pooled into his mouth, she whispered *'swallow it.'*

He ejaculated as he gulped, red semen pulsing forth, coating her lower belly and pubic hair.

His eyes widened as the portal opened, and his mind stepped into the stars.

5:6
"But what will we see?" the curious will ask.
"What awaits our immortal soul?"

CHAPTER 11

He was standing in a snowstorm.

He opened his arms wide, his hands high to feel the flakes as they landed upon him. It had been some time since he'd been out in snow, and this was an unexpected and pleasant surprise.

Opening his mouth, he stuck his tongue out and regretted it the moment a flake landed.

It wasn't snow but ash.

He spit the bitter residue from his mouth, but stopped when something off to his left squealed and scuttled away, moving too fast for him to see. In the distance a sickened soul let out an anguished cry.

No matter where he looked it was a shade of grey. Going from dark to light, the trees were void of color, the grass a charcoal palette.

Bianchi took a step, feeling a scorched flare under foot, looking, finding he was naked still, barefoot, walking across a bed of coals concealed below the embers that fell from a starless eon.

He stumbled over some rocks he'd not noticed, the ash making it hard for him to see defined shapes on the ground. Bianchi noticed the outline of a structure off to his left. After a few steps in that direction, he found he was standing before a house.

The house leaned ever so slightly, the weight of the dense ash covering the roof pushing it with an unseen hand.

The door was open a crack, a flickering light inviting him inside.

He stopped at the door, looking at the barren landscape that surrounded him. The blood that still coated him was congealed and sticky. He could feel each single flake of ash land on his matted hair, each impact a bee-sting prick of pain as a speck of hair was singed.

The wooden door offered resistance as he pushed it open, but he found solace that the interior was clear of the thickened soot.

"Hello?"

Whispered voices beckoned him further in. The blackness looked like an abyss of nothingness.

A candle flickered into life. The wick burned low, struggling to keep the utter darkness at bay.

He scanned the room, finding only a table adorned by the single candle. A step towards it scared a creature in the shadows. It shrieked before rushing into the world beyond through the open door.

A noise behind him caused Bianchi to jump. He turned, finding a new door he was positive hadn't been on that wall when he entered. Stepping forward, he turned the knob and opened it, finding only a black void staring back at him.

"Son?"

He heard the whispered word, but dared not believe it.

"Mom?"

"Oh son. How I've missed you. Please, get the candle, we're ever so cold."

He retrieved the candle from the table, ignoring the heat that touched his hand.

Stepping into the room, he found her on a bed, sitting up.

"Mom..."

She looked as only photos had shown him. Fifty years younger, vibrant, alive.

A step towards her brought another surprise; his father moving forth from the shadows. Walking.

"Dad?"

He'd never seen his father walk. The chair had always been part of him, as though a limb all of its own.

"Son," he said, wrapping Bianchi in a hug.

Naked and covered in blood, he should've felt awkward. But instead, he felt five years old again, being tucked into bed by his two loving parents.

"Why are you here?" he finally asked, breaking the embrace.

"You mustn't believe Father," his dad said, sitting on the bed beside his mom. Her face had changed. Her cheek was drooping on her left side, as though melting.

"He'll say what is necessary. Remember, sometimes it is ideal to be broken instead of repaired."

Another shadow shifted, and to Bianchi's surprise, McKay appeared, smiling at the man.

"The last I saw of you, you had a nail in the head," he said, before giving McKay a hug. For a man he'd known for a short period of time, it filled him with such joy to see him once again.

"Father used me, retrieved the box. Bianchi, the portal is open. The Black Heavens are awaiting his congregation."

The candle flickered, his father suddenly standing beside him, gently blowing on the flame.

"Don't blow it out dear," his mom said, "or *they'll* return."

"Just where *are* we?" Bianchi asked, only now noticing the artwork that hung on the walls. In each of them, a horned beast was being worshipped, reminding him of the carving on Abaddon's box.

"You are here."

"Where?"

"Ascended."

He stared at his father, understanding but not believing.

"Your blood allows you to travel across the void. Much like Hekate."

He stammered, trying to fully comprehend. He was in the Black Heavens. If his blood had allowed this travel, that meant only one thing.

"Father... is *my* father?"

His dad nodded, the pain etched across his face.

"Hekate...?"

"Yes. I'm sorry my boy. We did what we believed would open the cosmos for us. But it wasn't right. We ended up here, in this garden of depravity and pain."

"Are you all *here*? Or are you dead?"

A gust came through the door, dousing the flame, slamming Bianchi into pitch black. Panic and claustrophobia came full force, his breath hitching, his heart pounding. The shuffling of feet all around him rattled through the dark, *things* nearby, more than the three people he'd been speaking with.

A crash from the other room sounded, which immediately brought an image of the large table being overturned. A scratching noise came from beside his ear, and a flame at the end of a match burst to life. The candle was lit, and before Bianchi stood a massive beast. Towering over him, the creature stank of rancid meat. Saliva dripped from its mouth, the fluid slopping in coagulated puddles near Bianchi's feet.

"Why are you here?" the thing asked, it's snake-shaped head darting around as it asked the question. "You don't belong."

Bianchi looked past the beast, between its shoulders, the ends of sharp bone pierced its hide and membranous wings. He saw that the beings he'd believed were his parents and McKay had been replaced by three shadows, their shapes whirling as though infused with a tornado.

This was all one big deception.

"I'm here because Father sent me," he said, mustering as much courage as he could.

The monster roared with laughter, the sound shaking the floorboards below their feet.

"Father? That human masquerading as a God? As one of us? You bow to him?"

Bianchi shook his head, hoping that was the right response.

The beast smiled, exposing the triangular whites behind its scabbed lips.

"Come," it said, leaving the room, not waiting to see if Bianchi followed.

The other creatures hissed and growled. Even if Bianchi hadn't wanted to follow, he knew he couldn't stay in the darkened room. He'd be ripped to shreds.

He spotted the large creature just as it exited the house.

Bianchi got to the doorway but stopped, eyes returning to the ground.

"Come, human."

"My feet are bare. The coals will burn them."

The creature smirked, annoyed with his fragility.

"Just walk. We haven't time for pain."

Bianchi struggled to keep up with the brute. Its hoofed feet and long limbs allowed it to cover the ground with easy strides. He had to watch where his feet were landing, but his surroundings often distracted him. Occasionally he spotted a collared human on all fours, led like a dog by a black figure.

Was this where Father truly wanted to spend eternity?

Nothing but a barren, colorless world surrounded them as they moved. Every so often someone would scream, or a beast would let out a howl or growl, but more than anything, Bianchi saw lifeless body after lifeless body. Corpses sprawled out, surrounded by candles, or shapes drawn before them. People with slit wrists, or half of their head blown off, a discarded firearm nearby.

"Is this really the Black Heavens?" he asked the beast. Bianchi had studied this creature enough over the years to be confident it was Abaddon, but he couldn't bring himself to speak its name.

"It is. This battle has raged since the beginning of time. Man's hatred for his position, coupled with a desire for everlasting life, has brought us to this place time and time again."

"I saw a video of your heart being removed. Your horns being cut off. Did that actually happen?"

The beast let out a chuckle, looking off into the distance.

"Father has followed each step accordingly. This time at least. Yes, that was my heart and my horns. They will be in the sacred box. The energy that flows through me is eternal.

Those are merely physical devices for you humans to perform your odd rituals and incantations for ascendency. To stop Father, you know what needs to be done, don't you?"

Bianchi nodded, before they continued.

After another few minutes of walking, where they weaved through burned and blackened cadavers, Bianchi couldn't go on.

"Please stop. Please. My feet are badly burned. I can't walk anymore. My chest aches from breathing in all of this ash. I need to rest."

The demon stopped and turned, the look in his eyes that of pure hatred.

"Throughout time, men and women begged and pleaded for immortality. They did things no human should do to try to contact us. When we replied, they never liked the answer. This is where all cosmic chaos goes. Where all light ends. The Black Dragon that collided with the first particle of energy has created this plain for us to live for eternity. Your Father has looked into the abyss, seen the future, and accepted the Supreme Ruler of Emptiness as his Lord and Savior. Do you not wish to join him and Hekate for all eternity here?"

Something slithered around Bianchi's feet. The ground was covered in thousands of squirming serpents, their tongues darting in and out as they writhed over the coals.

"If this is the Black Heavens they covet, I would say no. Absolutely not."

A pain bloomed in his mid-section; warm fluid flowing from the area. He reached down, surprised to find a long knife protruding from his abdomen. He looked back at the demon, seeing it smiling at the violence.

"We'll meet again," it said, before Bianchi's vision shimmered. The grey of the other realm flickered and faded, and then he was standing in the commune again, the blood-rain still falling from above.

There stood Hekate, eyes wide. They both looked down again, her hand firmly grasped around the handle of the knife that had impaled him.

"You should learn to respect your elders," Father said through her, before Bianchi fell to the ground.

"He's waking."

Bianchi struggled to open his eyes, the light beyond his eyelids excruciating. Beeps and the humming of machines sounded nearby.

He reached out blindly with a hand, finding a handle and gripping it. He tried to sit.

"Easy, Bianchi," a man's voice said. Strong hands took hold of him, helping him up.

"Go get a nurse," they said. Footsteps sounded, growing distant as the person left the room.

"Nod if you can hear me."

He nodded.

"Do you know where you are?"

He shook his head, the effort feeling insurmountable.

That wasn't quite true. He had gathered that he was in a hospital, with the beeping and humming and the suggestion of getting a nurse. But just where he was, he couldn't say. He wasn't able to remember much of anything, which worried him.

"Take your time," a new voice said, a comforting tone to the man's timber. *This must be the nurse,* Bianchi thought, feeling the bed tilt behind his back to allow for a more comfortable sitting position.

"Professor Bianchi, my name is Reggie. I'm your nurse. Can you nod so that I know you heard me?"

He gave the man a nod, picturing a younger, taller male in his head. He tried again to open his eyes, but found he still couldn't.

"Hold on, we have your eyes taped shut. When you first arrived, after you were stabilized, you suffered a number of seizures."

Bianchi felt two quick stings as the tape was ripped from each eye, followed by bright light as they opened as though of their own accord.

Reggie stood beside the bed, leaning over to make sure his levels on the monitor looked correct. He'd been right about the man, dressed in crisp white with his name-tag on his left breast. He was tall, lean, and smiled warmly when they met eyes.

"Good to see you awake, Professor. You gave us all a scare."

Bianchi looked at the other two, recognizing them immediately as the detectives he'd spoken with after discovering McKay.

"You're lucky someone called in a check on your car."

The other detective stood and joined his partner at the end of the bed. He flipped open his notebook, taking a quick look, before closing it.

"What were you doing out in the middle of nowhere?"

Bianchi tried to speak, but a thousand tiny knives stabbed

his throat. A glass of water was placed almost immediately in his hand, the cold beverage feeling divine as he drank it. The first gulp sent a shockwave through his soul, a vision of blood, ash and pain exploding behind his present thoughts.

Reggie took the glass from him, setting it on the short table beside the bed.

"I'm going to go get the doctor overseeing your chart," he said. He turned to the detectives as he exited the room. "Please don't get him worked up."

"I don't remember anything," Bianchi said. The spoken words felt foreign, as though he were speaking in tongues.

"You were five miles north of Preacher's Rock when they found you. The area had been taped off previously, so you would've, what? Went under the tape, walked through that old commune, and just kept walking?"

Bianchi looked from one to the other.

"I went to the new commune. Where Father and his new group were living."

The two men broke into laughter.

"Look, if that hiker hadn't stumbled on your dust-covered car, you'd be dead right now. Our tracking dogs led us right to you. Were you distraught over what happened to McKay?"

Bianchi wasn't following.

He went to sit up straight and only then realized that his right arm was secured to the bed with handcuffs.

He rattled it a few times, as though testing to see the reality of them being there.

"What's this about?"

"Professor, we found you miles from a former cult commune, nude, with a large knife protruding from your stomach. You were covered in blood. *You* tell us why we'd have you handcuffed. Maybe we're worried you'd try to do something to yourself again?"

Bianchi looked down at this stomach, where thick, white bandages were taped in place. He turned to the machine beside him, watched the clear morphine drip let a small drop of pain meds flow into his system.

Hekate flashed in his mind, her smile, her nude body pressed against him, her mouth moving but Father speaking through her.

"No, I went to see Father. McKay was right about the old man surviving."

Both detectives shook their heads, doing a poor job of disguising the fact they felt sorry for him.

"Bianchi, we get it. You're under a lot of stress and grief is a tough pill to swallow. McKay's dead. It's been relayed to us that both of your parents passed away a few weeks back. That isn't news that's easy to take. For your own safety, we needed to make sure you didn't wake up and hurt yourself when no one was watching."

"My parents?"

"You didn't know? Ah, shit."

The man produced a key and unlocked the handcuffs, putting them into his jacket pocket. Bianchi wanted to rub the area the cuff had been on his wrist but decided to try and hold off. He didn't want to feel ashamed or have them pity him anymore.

"What about the tents and huts at the new commune?"

"There is no new commune. That's what we're trying to say. You were found in the literal middle of nowhere. You were in the dirt, bleeding to death."

"That can't be..."

The doctor and nurse returned. Reggie asked the detectives to wait outside. Instead, they mentioned they had to leave to follow up on some other cases. Before doing so, they told Bianchi to get well, and that they would be in touch.

It simply didn't make sense.

The doctor filled Bianchi in on his admission to the hospital, and that the knife had somehow not caused too much damage, missing everything important. When the doctor used the phrase *miracle* and *act of god*, Bianchi had to stifle a laugh.

His clothing had been found discarded nearby, which gave them his ID and parents' contact information. That was how their passing had been discovered.

"And there really was no commune out there?"

"Afraid not," the doctor said. "At least from what the detectives have told me. That's not really in my scope of practice."

Bianchi nodded, tuning the two medical professionals out. His mind was buzzing with trying to put the puzzle pieces back together. Something had happened. He knew that. Hekate was involved, as was Father.

A dark shadow came and went outside the hospital room window, dimming the sun for a fraction of a second. In that brief moment of darkened day, the ash covered world came roaring back into his consciousness, and it all clicked into place.

"When may I leave?" he asked, interrupting the doctor.

"You've been bedridden for sometime, so you may find your legs are not yet strong enough to support you. I'd think at this rate, a couple of weeks and you'll be able to go home."

Once he felt strong enough to stand and walk, he'd leave.

If the group really was going to ascend, it may have happened some time ago. But a part of him believed Father needed, or more accurately required, Bianchi to participate.

That was enough to motivate him.

For now he'd use this time to solve the riddle and figure out where Father may have gone.

11:1
Find solace through looking for the one true seal

CHAPTER 14

Two weeks later, and one month after being brought into the hospital, Bianchi was released.

He got dressed and said his goodbyes to Reggie. A cab was waiting outside, and he got in.

"Where too?" the driver asked.

"Preacher's Rock."

CHAPTER 15

"Forgive me, Father. For I have sinned."

The man stroked the thick, curly fur that grew along Father's legs. He let his hand travel up, until the back of his fingers grazed his shaft, then slid the hand down until it came to the hoof. He played with the rigid sheath of each half, watching as Father flexed it subconsciously.

"Your sins are forgiven," he said from his throne, motioning for Hekate.

She stepped forward, brandishing the chalice.

Father made a deft slit, the man's throat opening up like a broken dam, the blood cascading into the container held below.

The sacrifice slumped to the ground, body convulsing. Hekate handed the cup to the sickly looking savior, grinning like a schoolgirl as he poured the hot, frothy liquid into his mouth. Most of it splashed across his cheeks and beard, the white hair stained from the previous drinks.

He grotesquely licked his lips, then let out a contented sigh.

"How many more, dear?"

"Twenty-five, my Lord," she replied, while two servants dragged the dead man's body to the burning pit.

"Excellent."

That wretched puke Bianchi would be searching for them. Ascension had been delayed waiting for him. He was the last piece needed. His blood was key to letting Father step through completely and remain in the Black Heavens.

"He'll come," she said, tenderly touching his arm. He shrugged it off in disgust.

Bianchi would. The ritual was drawing to its conclusion.

Immortality awaited.

CHAPTER 16

Bianchi was confused.

The cab driver dropped him off as close to the rock as he was comfortable taking him, mumbling something about cursed grounds.

After walking to where the commune *should* have been, he stood in disbelief at the barren plain that he found. It was completely undisturbed land. Even if Father and his believers *had* lived here, there would surely be some sign of them left behind.

Think, damn it, he told himself, looking around the area for anything that would indicate where they'd gone or what he was supposed to do.

On his second spin trying to find anything of note, the haunting sobs of a woman crying caught his attention. He frantically searched the shrubs and surrounding trees, looking for the source.

The hitch of a hard cry made him feel sorrow so deep in his bones that he believed the universe was pulling him towards the Earth. His eyes shifted and caught on Preacher's Rock.

It was from there that the cries were coming.

He walked towards it, the woman's wails growing louder.

CHAPTER 17

Within the shadow cast by the large stone, Bianchi came upon a hideous figure pushing themselves up against the rock.

Her hair was matted with what he thought to be mud, but upon closer inspection was congealed blood.

She was rail-thin, her ribs protruding more than her deflated breasts. Where her nipples had been were now just two nubs of thickened scar tissue. From twenty feet away he could smell her, the filth dried around her legs. He had believed she was kneeling in the dirt, but when she spotted him and shifted, he realized her lower legs had been severed and cauterized. The rotting, charred flesh at the base of each limb suggested it hadn't happened that long ago.

"Miss?" he said, her eyes hauntingly empty of sanity.

He took a step towards her, and she let out an ear-piercing wail of terror.

"No, no, it's OK, shh, shh," he said, trying to show he meant no harm while ensuring he kept his distance. When he ran that thought through his head, he wasn't sure if he was keeping back to let her feel safe, or because he himself felt threatened and unsure of what she may do.

Bianchi stayed still. Her wailing grew in volume. Soon, he realized it had shifted from a pained cry to an unhinged, maniacal laugh. A grin spread across her face that only an insane person could pull off, her cheeks forced so wide that he thought her skin might split.

"You actually came?"

"I did," he replied, unsure of what her question meant.

"Is it Father you seek, or merely a way out?"

She started to lick her cracked lips, her tongue sliding between the folded flesh. A subtle shift forward where she used her arms to move her body towards him caused Bianchi to stumble backwards, his arms pinwheeling to keep his balance. He managed to stay on his feet, but glared at the woman as she laughed like some childish bully. He waited for her to say '*made you look,*' or '*you flinched,*' before punching his shoulder.

Instead, she stayed where she was, shifting her head like a cobra waiting for the perfect time to strike.

"I want to find Father. Is he speaking through you? Are those his deranged eyes I'm looking at?"

She let out another cackle, head thrown back with dramatic flair.

"I'm honored you'd believe Father would find me worthy enough to have him inside me. But it is just me. I have been left behind, to help you find them. That is, if you truly want to."

"Did Father do this to you?"

"Not with his own hands."

"How do I find him?"

"Do you remember your visit to the other side? Your walk

with one of our Lords? Look for a symbol beneath the rock. That symbol will unlock the door, and will lead you to where Father is waiting."

"I don't remember."

"You will," she said. Bianchi studied the walls around her, looking for anything else. He didn't notice the syringe she'd fished from where it was buried in the sand, never saw her plunge the needle into the stump of her leg until it was too late. Her mouth was frothing even before all of the syringe's contents had been injected into her body. She shook and convulsed, eyes bursting and ears bleeding.

Normally, Bianchi would've rushed to try and help her, but he knew. He knew she had no chance to be saved.

Against his moral judgement, he left her behind as he found the entrance below Preacher's Rock and began to descend.

10:3
To be guided from soil to stars, to be accepted
from solid to chaos

Bianchi had walked through the funeral parlour that lay beneath Preacher's Rock before. It was made up of a stone staircase that travelled along the wall until arriving at the rock floor. The light from the surface only extended down the steps so far, Bianchi fumbling in the dark until he made it to the bottom.

Once he had finished taking the steps, a dozen candles burst to life around the chamber, illuminating the space adequately, but not enough to fully share the secrets lurking in the shadows.

A stone table lay in the middle, an empty coffin on top. McKay had said that when he was down here he'd found the body with the cow's head. The lid to the box was pushed off to the side furthest from Bianchi.

Somewhere nearby, water dripped, the sound amplified by the stillness of the air.

Each time Bianchi had been in here, a coffin had always been in place, but he'd never been able to work up the courage to look within. It hadn't mattered whether he was a child or not. This had been merely a chamber to pass through from one area to the next.

Now, he needed to look for something that would lead him to Father, a symbol or sign that would direct his search.

The chamber was old. Bianchi's academic mind was stunned while taking in everything carved and painted on the walls. He'd never once spent the time to investigate the rest of the area, and realized that if he had, he might not be so panicked while trying to find the *thing*. He'd most likely know where it was already. But as such, he didn't have a clue.

As he began to search the wall beside him a loud thunk came from behind. He whirled around, finding no one and nothing in the space. Bianchi stayed still, waiting to see if it happened again. He didn't have to wait long. Almost immediately the wooden coffin bounced where it lay with a thunk.

Something made a noise from within, a blur of movement detected for the briefest of moments along the edge of the wood. A thin, scaled *thing* elongated and looped over the edge of the coffin before sliding back into the space that Bianchi couldn't see. For that he was thankful. The coffin bounced again.

He felt a presence. Warm breath on his neck, the swish of a tail. He spun around to find he was still alone as the coffin clattered again.

"*Bianchi,*" a woman said from a dark corner as one of the candles snuffed out.

"*Bianchi,*" it repeated, three more candles going dark.

While the coffin rattled around the table some more, Bianchi took it as a sign that he needed to hurry up and look for a symbol. He scanned the walls, letting his hands travel across the surface, feeling for something to alert him that he'd found what he was supposed to.

Whoever was in the corner thankfully stayed there, their wheezing and raspy breathing causing him to continually glance towards where they crept.

After skimming over the walls, he took a deep breath and started over. His nerves were rattled, preventing him from having the necessary patience to look at every piece that adorned the chamber walls.

His eyes passed over odd symbols, unknown and unrecognizable letters and words, until finally he spotted something that was distinct.

A dragon.

Looking closely at it, Bianchi saw that it had been carved into the wall and painted over at some point. A foot long, the ink had faded so that the shape of the body was visible but only a few scales remained. The head was what cemented it for him. The eyes burned into him as though they were real. He found his hand was moving of its own volition, caressing the mighty serpent's shape, before his finger tip caught an edge. The coffin rattled harder, the thing inside thrashing around. He pushed against it and the outline of the beast illuminated, as though a light switch had been flipped.

"*Yes...*" the voice said from the corner, before all of the candles went out. The only light now was the symbol on the wall. The beast within the coffin hit the wood hard enough that the box crashed off the stone table, slamming to the floor.

Bianchi looked towards the coffin, unable to see anything in the darkness. He could hear the approaching sound of slithering scales on the stone. A click from the wall got his attention.

Turning, he saw the shape glow.

He shielded his eyes as the brightness intensified. He could hear a hum, a vibration through his bones, and then...

Bianchi was standing in a forest.

9:3
Travel through and across the celestial acreage

"He is here, my Lord," the young woman said.

Father nodded, a sly grin spreading on his face.

He'd known Bianchi was smart, but worried he wouldn't connect the dots.

"I'm so very happy."

He motioned for her to leave.

The group he'd brought with him, deep into the mountains in the Todzhinsky District in Russia, were prepared for what was to come.

Pain. Pleasure. Ascension.

The time had arrived for Father to perform the final transformative steps in the ritual within the circular ruins. Every piece of the puzzle had fallen into place. Now all that was left was for Bianchi to arrive, and the final sacrament would occur.

Father smiled wider now, the last dregs of sanity flowing from his soul.

Just where the fuck was he?

Bianchi had walked aimlessly for two hours, searching for any sign of civilization, or Father and the group. He'd seen nothing, not even a trail that he would consider man-made.

He was able to see a high mountain range off to one side, but he'd never been someone to know which way North was, so he couldn't be confident in direction he was heading, or what way the mountains travelled.

Bianchi assumed that Father would be near. Why else would the symbol he pressed bring him here?

He looked at his watch, seeing the display read 6:32PM.

The sun was dropping, the light beginning to fade. The mountains were closed in around him enough that it would grow dark soon.

Finding a place to spend the night would be key. He had no food, or anything to make a fire with, but if he could find a tree to climb or an alcove to protect him from the elements, that would be ideal. Bianchi wasn't outdoorsy or someone who camped in a tent, so he was well aware he was out of his comfort zone.

Taking in the area, he decided he'd keep walking towards the mountain range, looking for a tree to climb. Not knowing exactly where he was meant he wasn't sure what animals might lurk when the sun went down.

He walked for another thirty minutes, his anxiety continuing to increase as the sun dipped lower, when he spotted something odd on a tree a few meters ahead.

Pushing through some underbrush, he saw that he was looking at an old wooden sign nailed to a tree.

It had a strange etching on it, which he thought was an attempt to draw horns, an arrow pointing to his left and a word in a language he thought might be Russian.

"Сюда"

"What does it mean?" he asked the forest. He knew some Russian, but this word was unfamiliar.

The arrow, for him, was the smoking gun.

"This way?" he said, trying to lessen his tension by speaking aloud.

He stepped over a downed tree and saw a rocky path that appeared as though it was placed and not random. At first he was excited. Finding a path to walk on would be far easier than having to bushwack through the forest like he had been. But then he realized this path led somewhere, most likely to where Father would be waiting, which struck him with an unanticipated foreboding.

Bianchi had walked down the path a short distance when he noticed something else ahead on the stones. Taking a closer look, he saw that there were symbols carved into some of the rocks. This was all the sign he needed. He carried on, knowing that he was getting closer and closer to finding Father's location.

This madness needed to end. Father had to be stopped.

CHAPTER 22

"He is following the pathway, Father. Bianchi will be here tomorrow."

Father nodded at Hekate.

His eyes darted over the sleeping parishioners.

"Andrew," he said, snapping his fingers.

A thin, teen boy sat up slowly, looking at his leader.

"Go, find Bianchi. Lead him to me."

The boy grabbed a crudely fashioned wooden crutch from the ground and used it to stand. His left leg took his weight, the useless, beastial appendage on his right not yet accepting the human host.

He limped out of the structure slowly, shuffling along with the crutch.

"We need to transform five more tonight," Father said, after a few moments. "Choose five and bring them to the rock."

CHAPTER 23

Bianchi was exhausted.

He'd followed the stone pathway for another hour, well past when the sun had set. He could hardly see five feet in front, the darkness enveloping everything. He'd had to slow to a crawl, wanting to make sure he stayed on the path.

Now, the lack of food, water, and sleep had caught up, and he sat down in the middle of the path.

He knew this wasn't a good place to rest, but he couldn't fight it anymore. His eyes started to close, the battle to keep them open futile. His head nodded and bobbed as he struggled to stay awake, before finally his chin dipped and he slumped to the ground, fast asleep.

CHAPTER 24

The strangest of noises woke Bianchi.

It sounded like a foot step followed by a stick tap.

He shook his head, trying to rid his brain of the exhausted fog that gripped his grey matter. Rolling onto his side, his back and hips ached from sleeping on the rocky ground.

He blinked a few times, letting his eyes adjust to the low morning light. He spotted the figure moving towards him on the path.

"Bianchi," the male said, his age tough to determine from where he sat. "Father requests a meeting."

Bianchi gave a nod, before getting to his feet.

"Who are you?"

He could see now that the man was a teenager. Sixteen, maybe seventeen. He couldn't bring himself to look at the animal limb that hung from below the bottom of his cut-off pants.

"Just a disciple. My name means nothing."

Bianchi chuckled hearing this. The blind devotion

towards a madman. He wouldn't be surprised if this teen had been servicing Father's sexual desires already. The old man had no limits. Worse now that he believed he was an actual living, breathing God.

"Father makes a lot of promises, doesn't he?"

The boy matched Bianchi's gaze a moment before turning and hobbling back down the pathway.

"You think you're going to the Black Heavens?"

"I know I will. I don't think it. I've been chosen. My transformation has begun. Even now I feel a pulse starting deep within my new form."

Bianchi hadn't yet started following the teen. He was saddened that this young man had been tricked into being a guinea pig for the crazy leader.

"I've been to the Black Heavens. Trust me when I say this. You don't want to go."

That halted the teen's shuffle. He turned and looked at Bianchi, his face a mix of shock and awe.

"You have?"

Bianchi just smiled, knowing the hold he had over him now.

"I have. It's a horrible place, filled with beasts and ash. Darkness and death. It is not a paradise, nor is it somewhere you'd want to spend eternity."

"That's because you don't believe. Father said that non-believers will never see the true form of the Black Heavens. If I had a knife I'd butcher you where you stood," he said, before spitting near Bianchi's feet.

"Look kid, Father says a lot of things. That's what crazy men do. That's how he convinces you it's ok to fuck your ass or for you to suck his dick. Or, even *more insanely*, let healthy people have their legs cut off and an animal's leg sewn on. Just shut up and take me to your leader."

The two walked without speaking for some time, the only sound the crutch hitting the stones. Bianchi didn't care about the symbols on the path, or the lifeless limb with the atrophied hoof. He wanted this to come to an end. Father had done far too much damage to far too many people. How that meant he deserved reverence and immortality was beyond Bianchi.

They made their way along the winding trail, the forest opening up into a valley. Across a river, Bianchi could see a stone structure with what looked to be chimney smoke puffing from the top. Some distance to the right was a raised section of land with stone slabs standing on end, forming a circle. Immediately he felt a chill when he saw the ruins.

"Where are we?"

"The final place before ascension. Abaddon's Circle."

Bianchi remembered seeing something similar carved on the top of Abaddon's box.

"No, I mean, where in the world are we?"

"Russia."

He was in Russia. Bianchi was stunned. The symbol he'd found under Preacher's Rock had transported him halfway around the world.

Many pieces of his research were falling into place. Now, he just needed to end the false prophets reign and destroy Abaddon's heart and box.

He let out a long breath, before walking to catch up.

As they approached the partially collapsed structure that the group called home, a woman exited the building, the flames above her head shooting a dozen feet into the air.

"Hekate," he said, which caused the boy to look once more at Bianchi.

"You know her name?"

"Of course," he said, walking ahead of the teen.

"She's my sister."

CHAPTER 25

When they arrived at the building, a group of haggard looking followers had made their way out to see Bianchi. Some didn't believe he was actually there, others wanted to see him for the first time, in the flesh.

The boy went to six people gathered over to one side and immediately began talking to them animatedly. They kept looking at Bianchi, before talk would start again, the teen having excited them when he shared Bianchi's relationship.

Bianchi knew that most were looking at him with fervor and lust. Not sexually, but with a deep joy that he would be sacrificed, and the Black Heavens would open. He had no desire to take his own life, but he understood that Father had been preaching that to them for some time. It was what was expected of him.

Hekate walked to Bianchi, stopping a dozen feet away. Bianchi felt his face flush with shame, knowing what had occured the last time he'd seen her.

"Bianchi. We are so pleased you've found us."

"Sure made it easy, didn't you?"

She grinned at him, as though his brush with death in the desert was all a game, a joke played by siblings.

"Father is waiting."

She didn't wait for a reply, leaving him where he stood with the expectation he would follow. As he walked after her, he felt like a scolded child or a dog who had been told to go fetch a stick.

The stench of the congregation's rot hit him as soon as they entered the remains of the building.

In the middle of the floor, the remaining parishioners sat in various stages of decay. Some still had their legs, while others had suffered a surgical transplant of one or both limbs. In one corner, corpses of the dead animals were stacked, the liquid that pooled below them a dark red. In the far corner to Bianchi's right, some of the flock squatted, shitting. Their crude DIY latrine buzzed with flies and writhed with maggots.

Bianchi puked, unable to hold back in this squalor.

Hekate handed him a dirty cloth, and he muttered thanks as he used it to wipe his face and hands. He offered it back, but she motioned for him to discard it, so he tossed it among the waste on the ground.

Bianchi spotted Father perched on yet another makeshift throne.

What greeted him this time was far from pleasant.

Father sat, propped up by a severed head, his hoofed legs splayed out obscenely. His genitals had been removed, a mutilated festering wound remaining. Bianchi saw no attempt at treatment on the area. One of his arms had been cut off, replaced with the limb of an animal. He suspected a bear, but from a distance, he couldn't be certain. The old man's gaunt chest was stained and crusted with blood, as was his neck. Another horn had been affixed to his chin, an attempt to match the two that sprouted from his forehead.

The man's eyes blazed when he saw Bianchi.

"Come, my *son*," Father said, beckoning Bianchi towards him with his human hand.

"Look at you," Bianchi said, once he was standing a few feet before the throne. "What have you done to yourself?"

Father smirked.

"You can't see the greatness? You truly are stupid."

"Hekate's fire, that I see. That scares me and impresses me. You? You look like you're moments from death. A pretender to the throne."

Father's eyes darted from Bianchi to Hekate and back. It dawned on Bianchi. Father couldn't see her true form.

"You're a fraud. You can't even see her fire?"

He knew he was poking the beast and Father might erupt, but he wanted to try and push the old man, force him into exposing a weakness.

"I have no need to answer such an ungrateful cunt. We gave you every opportunity to join us and stand by our side as we ascend. Tomorrow, we will fulfill the prophecy that was foretold and make our way to the Black Heavens."

Bianchi wanted to laugh at the old man, but before he could, Hekate shifted beside him and he felt a blinding pain through his head.

He stumbled backwards, landing on his knees in the filth and feces. Bianchi lifted a hand dripping with waste to his head, sobs coming hard when he felt the nail protruding from his forehead.

"Whaaad doooo daaattt feeeerrr," he tried to say, but failed.

Hekate stood before him while Father leaned forwards on his throne, the two grinning like Cheshire cats.

"Ascendency awaits the holy, not the sinners. You'll play your part, don't you worry."

Arms wrapped around his own, his protests useless as he was dragged away.

Bianchi was ripped from his stupor by a horrendous beast growling in the dark.

"You're awake."

He rolled over, finding himself on a soft mattress in an expansive bed.

"Where am I?"

"Your mom's bedroom."

"But it doesn't stink?"

"I've cleaned."

The creature stepped forth from the dark shadows. Bianchi looked away.

"Do I scare you, Bianchi?" it asked with a chuckle.

"To my core."

"I'm not here to hurt you. I'm here to walk you through what's to come."

Bianchi got off the bed, seeing the room as it used to be. "Well?"

The beast smiled and motioned for him to follow. It

opened up the door and they stepped into the world of ash and decay.

It was as Bianchi remembered. Dead bodies, humans in chains, and hideous monstrosities acting out their darkest perversions.

"I got spiked."

The creature stopped and looked at Bianchi. He could see it was trying to formulate a tactful response. In an odd way, he respected this.

"You did. I'm sorry. When I return you, you'll have limited function. But that doesn't mean you can't help me stop Father."

"Why do you want him stopped? Isn't this a direct pipeline for you to fuck humans and eat flesh?"

Anger flashed across its grotesque face, before it calmed.

"Father is *not* a God. He has no business getting this close to true immortality. We've had others ascend throughout history. But none of them have gone to these lengths. He has created his own congregation. His own legion of servants. The transplants and bloodletting have impressed our mother, the Black Dragon. But for a new God to ascend, one of us will need to be relieved. "

"Ah, I get it. Father possesses your heart, your horns. Your box. If he ascends, you are sent to earth?"

"Close. Your intelligence has always impressed. If Father truly ascends, because he possesses my essence, I will be jettisoned into the far reaches of the universe. Chaotic energy with no home."

"What's in it for me?"

"Yes, the eternal question you humans always ask. For you, salvation. A life of sorts without Father. I have the power to undo the damage caused by the nail. I can reset your brain. You'll live out your days."

"What about my parents?"

"Dead."

"You can't bring them back?"

The beast burst into laughter, the sound like nails on a chalkboard.

"That is but a fairy tale concept. This is real life. Dead is dead. I can undo the damage because of our connection. That is it. But you'll see them again."

He gave a nod.

"How do I know you're telling the truth?"

"A beast such as I never tells the truth. You'll just need to trust in the process."

The creature continued walking, Bianchi discovering it was harder and harder to breathe. The air was thick and hot, the ash making his eyes itch and burn.

"Almost there," it said, pointing ahead.

Bianchi saw the circular ruins, shrouded in a red casing of stained glass windows.

"I had the ruins built here in the Black Heavens and on Earth. A way to have cosmic connectivity. To humans it may appear as though it is a portal, but the truth is, it is a doorway that only I control."

The weight of what the beast said caught in Bianchi's chest.

"So, you can open and close this at will?"

"Yes."

"Why don't you just keep it closed? Or is it open because you need your heart and horns back?"

"That was how Father opened the door to begin with. Since then, he has been trying to transform himself into one of us, a cosmic deity. Yes, I do need to retrieve those items you speak of. But more importantly, I need to stop his advances and prevent the door from staying open. When he called forth Sheol and myself, in the basement of their church, it forced me to look at just *what* was happening. Father had only found lesser openings in spaces of the dark realm. The ruins are the true doorway."

CHAPTER 27

They paused at the edge of a pond, filled with bubbling lava and stinking of sulphur. A creature with a dozen wings and as many heads was picking up humans and throwing them far out into the fiery liquid, their screams piercing the darkness.

"What do I need to do?" Bianchi asked.

Abaddon smiled, showing the depths of the universe in his gaping maw.

Father led the remaining parishioners towards the stones that made up Abaddon's sacred circle.

He leaned heavily on his wooden crutch, Hekate doing her best to keep him upright.

Father glanced at her, eyes narrowing, wondering if the flames Bianchi alluded to were real. He felt no warmth.

The sickly and the decayed moaned and groaned from behind, the group's ranks thinning as the days progressed. It was of no importance to him. The Black Heavens awaited, and soon they'd be nothing more than stepping stones long faded from his memory.

Once they'd climbed the steps, Father had the robed members adorn their faces with their masks, ensuring the cosmic gods were represented.

"The time of ascendency has arrived!"

His words reverberated through the gathered, orgasmic moans replying to his baritone.

"We shall awaken our true forms from slumber. I, as your

Lord, bow before the Black Dragon! Open your mighty wings and accept us into your loving grace."

A ragged wind rushed through the congregation, a summoning scream pierced through the sky.

"Bring him forth."

Bianchi was dragged by two men, the group parting to let the trio through. His head lolled back and forth, his tongue hanging from his mouth. The nail was still embedded in his forehead.

"Lay him on the stone slab."

Hekate helped to position Bianchi. The man simply groaned, his limbs remaining limp.

"Our lamb has returned home. Now, I call upon Abaddon, the Great. Abaddon the Horned One. To open the gates to the Black Heavens and allow us eternal passage and immortality!"

Clouds formed, the sky opening and rain beginning to fall. The members huddled closer together as they were soaked. Still, their chanting didn't diminish.

Father swayed with his one arm raised high.

Bianchi was aware of what was happening, but unable to do anything. He felt the drool pool along his lips before spilling over and dribbling down the side of his face. The rain peppered his forehead, a snapping bite of pain happening each time a larger drop connected with the implement sticking out of his head.

As the clouds swirled and the sun was blotted out, a darkness rolled over the circular ruins.

The stench of ash and rot told Bianchi that the beast had arrived. He could hear the gasps and murmurs when the creature stepped forth between the stones.

Bianchi shed a single tear knowing what was to come.

All around him the world flickered, from forest to stained glass windows.

CHAPTER 29

Father spoke the words needed to ascend.

"Before there was light, before there was dark, there was only chaos! Energy unharnessed, awaiting a destination. When the dust is settled and the scorned have been eradicated, man, woman, and child shall stand shoulder-to-shoulder with hoof and horn!"

The parishioners dropped to their knees, sobbing at the reverence of the words.

"The great mass will begin, the chosen walking as one, hoofed and horned. For I, our savior, have spoken the gospel and the gates have opened and await. The Black Heavens greet all with chaos and pain!"

Everything happened in the blink of an eye.

Lightning flashed, thunder roared, the congregation screaming and rushing around in a panic.

Abaddon swooped over, slamming one of its immense clawed hands down on Bianchi's head. Not only was the nail driven deep into his brain, but the force shattered his skull. Brain matter, piss, and shit burst out of his openings.

Father's eyes went wide seeing his son's body convulse and spasm.

Hekate let out a scream while the other parishioners tried to rush away.

Abaddon's tail lashed out, removing half of the heads with one swipe.

A flash of fire blasted around it, Hekate having focused her rage on the beast.

Father flickered and started to disappear, his body half in the Black Heavens, half on Earth.

Abaddon sent its tail out once more, cutting the remaining parishioners in half. As they dropped like flies, it let out a ferocious bellow.

Hekate stepped in front of it once again. Abaddon wasted no time, pouncing and ripping. Her head was tossed aside with no care. Her body flopped across Bianchi's still twitching legs.

Abaddon took two long strides, grabbed the box from where Father had set it, and retrieved the heart and horns from within. Stuffing the heart into its mouth, it ate greedily, watching Father's form writhe in pain.

The beast then took one horn and stabbed it into Father's chest. The other he stabbed into one of Father's animal legs.

An immense explosion occurred, rocking the Russian wilderness.

As the dust settled, Abaddon remained standing.

The lower half of Father's body lay nearby.

Bianchi's remains had been thrown from the slab. Abaddon crouched near the man, whispering to the body.

"Bianchi. I do apologize. A demon never tells the truth. May your cosmic soul rejoice and be free. I'll ensure you're comfortable."

CHAPTER 29

A shadow eclipsed the light above, a deafening roar forcing the animals nearby to run for cover. Abaddon looked up at the shape of the black dragon as it slithered across the atmosphere.

The beast closed its eyes and let its mind go dark, before returning to the Black Heavens.

11:9
For the red will shine down on thee and those anointed

Father awoke to a landscape covered in ash.

All around him were screams of pain.

He looked down, yelling in terror. The lower half of his body was missing.

He tried to crawl, but with only one usable arm, couldn't.

A crunching sound from his left got his attention.

Looking over, he saw Abaddon standing beside him.

"Hey, preacher man. Look at you? Actually in the Black Heavens. How do you like it? Everything you dreamed it would be?"

A vicious roar from nearby caused the man to wince, the caked blood on his face doing little to dispel how scared he was.

"Take care, Father. You won't last long. But you have made it farther than most. We'll give you that."

Abaddon turned and walked to a nearby house, entering the structure and closing the door.

Father was about to yell at the creature when he felt

something sniffing beside him. Looking, he saw a beast that resembled a dog. The thing's snout was rolled back like a flower, its fangs wide and ready to latch onto him.

He managed to let out a plea for help before his jugular was ripped wide open.

The sounds of children laughing got Bianchi's attention.

Sitting at a table in a room, he struggled to remember anything. *Why was he there? Where exactly was he? Who were these people sitting across from him?*

One by one, their faces came to him, as did their names.

McKay.

Mom.

Dad.

Hekate.

"What are we all doing here?" he asked, feeling lethargic.

He turned to look at his sister, seeing another man sitting beside her.

"Who is that?"

The man smiled, his face a twisted painting of wood, burned flesh and dripping visera.

"You don't recognize me?"

Bianchi shook his head. He felt like he should, but couldn't.

Hekate took his hand in hers, while she stroked his forearm with her other hand. She looked sad. Aged. As though she'd just gone through a monumentally hard time in her life.

His mom was sobbing now, his dad trying to console her.

McKay babbled to himself, the words not making any sense and often spoken too low for Bianchi to even hear.

"That's Brad," Hekate whispered to him finally.

Bianchi looked at his former childhood friend. He thought of McKay's notes on what they suspected had happened.

"So, why are we all here?"

The others stared at Bianchi as though he should already know.

All around them the sounds of children laughing grew louder, before the noise shifted and Bianchi realized it wasn't children at all but the sounds of beasts screaming from outside somewhere.

The room developed a red hue above them. Looking, Bianchi saw they were encased under a layer of crimson stained glass.

"*No.* It can't be?"

Leaving the others at the table, he left the room, exiting at the end of an isle. Rows of pews led from where he stood to the altar at the end.

Behind the altar was a massive stone statue.

Bianchi dropped to his knees as the familiar taste of acrid ash filled his mouth and the scent of sulphur invaded his nose.

The likeness of Abaddon looked down upon the man.

Knowing he would be here forever filled Bianchi with dread and sorrow.

CHAPTER 31

Outside, beasts bellowed, creatures roared and the wayward souls screamed in terror.

END.

And here we are.

This is going to be an afterword possibly unlike any you've read before. Consider this more of an essay than an afterword. A 'Why I wrote the Father of Lies Trilogy' essay. I know it's been something many readers have asked about. They wanted to know more of the 'why' and the 'what.'

On October 1st, 2019, I released 'Ritual' on an unsuspecting world. Initially, it was meant as a stand alone story. A brief slab of brutality and depravity. I've mentioned before that it came from two pieces merged into one. A detective story at the end that was slotted onto the cult story at the start. But the cult story arrived from something I was knee deep in. And when I had a few people mention, most specifically Diamond and Sonora, that they wanted more, I knew that what I was working on and researching would work perfectly to continue the story. So, I did. I vomited forth the second book 'COMMUNION' before working on this, the third release, 'Sacrament.'

I personally loved the three act flow. From Brad to McKay to Bianchi. We get three different males, all used by Father, to try and reach his end goal – ascension to the Black Heavens.

Before I dive into the backstory of writing the novellas, here's a quick "what's next?" in this world. And while we've seen the ending arrive and Abaddon has closed the doorway for Father and imprisoned Bianchi's soul within the chapel devoted to Abaddon's worship in the Black Heavens, I knew this was a cult/cyclical tale.

At some point in 2021, the Father of Lies Omnibus will arrive, which will feature a novellette included called 'Eucharist' which will hopefully make those who've enjoyed this trilogy happy. As well, I've created the Book of Lies. Father's Bible if you will.

Now, regarding this trilogy.

I've always been intrigued by the darker aspects of life. One such thing is the dark web. That "mythical" part of the world wide web that hosts many horrible things.

Part of what inspired my deeper dive into the dark web was Jon, the singer of Dissection. Their album Reinkaos was based on the Liber Azerate, a tome that featured the ramblings of The Temple of the Black Light (previously known as MLO or Misanthropic Luciferian Order). While there are numerous parts of this cult that are homophobic, racist, sexist etc etc, I was intrigued with their search for cosmic chaos immortality. Granted a lot of what they've written in the Liber Azerate is plucked from other sources, even Lovecraft lore, the overall desire to open the cosmic gates and bring forth the Black Dragon was intriguing. In fact, through initial message boards on the 'normal' internet, I found some comments that suggested Jon did ascend when he killed himself, having successfully completed the ritual. Now, I obviously can't speak to if he did or did not, but through one such message board, I connected with a singer who has performed for a number of black metal bands (no, I won't name them) who stated that if I was truly seeking out the way to ascend, they could direct me to a dark web group that believed they were following Jon's footsteps and that The Temple of the Black Light had successfully conjured demons and opened up pathways to the next realm.

Color me fucking intrigued.

In the fall of 2018, I was finally able to access, through a VPN and a Tor browser, this group. It was not easy nor pretty. In fact, for the first four months I was considered filth and I was not allowed to ask questions, I was only allowed to answer them. They had steps in place to ensure I was truthfully seeking enlightenment. I never once hid that I was looking for inspiration for writing, but I knew they would make sure it wasn't going to be an easy time.

I'm going to stop here and say – if you're actually squeamish, (which would surprise me if you got to this point in this trilogy and you were!) you may want to skip over some of the next pieces I'm going to discuss.

Intiation.

The group had three leaders, all males, who governed over their flock. Father Sheol, Father Abaddon and Father Belial. Three of the eleven cosmic chaos Gods. They stated that all three lived with and served their 'mother' who they referred to as the Black Dragon. This was all pretty much word for word from the Liber Azerate and I found none of it shocking.

It was the necessary 'things' they wanted people to do to work up the ladder to ensure they'd ascend that I found repulsive and grotesque. And I grew up with Consumption Junction, Live Leak and Goatse.

Of the requested 'acts' I was only willing to perform one of them, which was a video taped act of self-bloodletting. In this instance, I filmed myself making a small cut on my forearm which drew blood. Very minor compared to the other bloodletting I watched occur and that were uploaded. If I was unwilling to do this act, I would not be granted permission to enter the message board again. One act of bloodletting that I objected to doing, which resulted in two more weeks of being considered filth, was to cut along the erect penis and masturbate to conclusion using the blood as lubrication. Hey, I warned you this wasn't pretty. Other acts they requested members to go – animal sacrifice, bloodletting of others etc, were all horrible acts.

The members of this group truly believe that they're near completion of their own personal ascendency journeys and as such, the group started with three leaders and when I last logged in, was down to one. The other two having 'ascended.' If you've read between the lines, you'll understand that this means they've taken their own lives and left this world.

The mental health issues between the members were incredibly fascinating. I'm not trained in any sort of area to diagnose or discuss in any depth what was going on with these members, but time and time again, with the hopes that the Black Dragon would darken their souls and pick them to ascend, they'd do horrible things to themselves or others to appease the Gods. Cutting off nipples. Removing a finger. Arson, assault, whatever it was that they believed the order would see as an act to move them closer to being chosen, they would do it.

Close to four years and over 400 hours in this message group (I'd usually spend an hour in the group every second or third day for my sanity) I'd seen a lot. Stuff I'd wished I'd never seen.

But it was a series of photos and a short video that Father Abaddon shared in early 2020 that absolutely rocked me. I've actually described a bit of it in COMMUNION. In the series of photos and in the video, it is purported that while Father Abaddon is engaged in sexual relations with Black Dragon, something arrives in the corner of the room and watches. At one point, it steps closer to the light and reaches a large, thick hand towards Black Dragon. This woman is on her hands and knees, Father Abaddon behind her. He is flagellating her with something that has sharp ends on it as her back is torn open and bloody. She appears to notice this figure first and reaches out with one hand. The video ends when they touch hands.

Is it real? Doubt it. Is it real? Possibly?

This was in a run down apartment where they lived in squalor, most likely squatting. Father Abaddon was filming this (so they say) for their own gratification. The photos were screenshots of the video and didn't do much to enhance what it was that arrived there, but I will say – in one frame there is nothing, in the next *something*. It is one of the few times I've seen something online that actually scared the absolute shit out of me.

The video and pictures unnerved me – it made me rethink how much more I wanted to visit and deal with these people. I continued to visit over the fall and into winter but as I wrapped up writing this, I slowed. Over the last three months, I've only gone back a handful of times, more out of curiosity than anything. The group seems to be growing in numbers, most members live in Europe from what I gather, based on their accents and other things that tip me off, give me that impression.

It's an extreme group and frankly, in order for me to make any more headway or move up the ladder, I would need to do more extreme things and that's not where I'm at or who I am. Selfish to think, but I got what I wanted from it and I'm fine with that. There is an odd pull, though. Knowing what they're attempting to do. I can't guarantee I'll never go back. My mind keeps asking – was that real? Rationally I know it shouldn't be, but I also love Bigfoot videos and Lake Monster videos.

I'll wrap this up so that I don't begin to ramble.

This trilogy was written with the main narrative of a cult led by a deranged leader. What someone will do to get what they want, by any means necessary. In Father's case, he believed he needed to take on the visual appearance of his Gods. Yes, I did see someone attempt to remove part of themselves and attach an animal part. That person suffered an infection and I gathered they died from it, not wanting to go to the hospital. The lengths people will go for power and the lengths others will go to follow. It's an insane world. But it always has been. More of it is just now coming out into the light.

I'd like to thank everyone who took this trilogy for a cruise. Even those one star reviewers. You may have given Ritual a one star review and questioned why you read it, but I bet some parts of that novella have stayed with you. For those who carried on, I hope I did the story justice. I know the research I was doing kept me plugged in and dare I say it, excited to see where Father, Bianchi, Hekate and Brad ended up. McKay too.

Thank you to Mason McDonald for the cover art. He captured it all so well. From the bleak cover of Ritual, to the flames of Chaos pushing around McKay on COMMU-NION and now to the red Church of Abaddon on Sacrament, you've nailed each piece.

Thank you to David Sodergren for your help with all of this. You're a good friend.

Thank you to Ross Jeffery for the formatting and feedback.

To Diamond and Sonora – you two have been champions of this brutality. Thank you.

Gavin – your friendship and support have been instrumental. Thank you.

Amanda, Auryn and OJ – you're the three best friends that anybody could have. Love you.

This trilogy was written completely while listening to Dissection and Dimmu Borgir. Dissection played a vital role, through their lyrics and music in inspiring me and forcing me to investigate the meaning behind the words. I say that while also stating – I do not condone Jon's (and the other band members) views. I wish it would go without saying, but I believe it needs to be and is necessary. Dissection had some very extreme views (just Google Jon and see if you must) and I share none of them. I'd also like to say, that as far as I can tell – neither does Dimmu Borgir for the most part. Satanist world view, sure, but I've not come across an interview or article where they've discussed hatred for LGTBQ, POC etc.

In closing, I want to thank you all for the continued support for my work and this trilogy. It has meant the world.
Until we meet again,
Steve
Edmonton, AB
January 13, 2021.

EUCHARIST
BONUS NOVELETTE

EUCHARIST

Slinging on her pack, Anna took one more look at her watch.

Seven on the dot.

Good, she thought, she'd get to her camp site in eight hours, get the tent set up and have plenty of time to review data before it got dark.

Anna worked for the Saint Petersburg State University. She was an arborist, researching tree growth and development. Working on her PHD thesis, she was determined to prove that her chosen land area had battled a plague over five hundred years ago. The three hour drive always felt long, first thing Saturday morning, but it was worth it for her education.

This was to be her last data collection hike of the season, October effectively signaling that it was time to analyze her hundreds of samples she'd collected over the last few months. She loathed spending time in front of a microscope, but knew it was a necessary evil.

She'd also be collecting the micro SD cards from game cameras for her roommate, Igor. Igor was working on a few running theories of his own. What exactly? She didn't know. But she was to review the footage and mark off any animal sightings of note on the playback.

Eight hours of hiking ahead. Eight grueling hours of collecting her samples and Igor's cards. Then set up, review, sleep, and pack up. Then eight hours back.

She hated it and loved it at the same time.

At least she'd be outdoors. The leaves now orange and yellow, the air cooling slightly from the brutal summer heat she'd been dealing with on the prior treks in.

She always marveled at how peaceful she felt while out here. It was as though a part of her had a connection with Gaia, the earth's pulse flowing through her muscles. Even during this time of the year, familiar sounds greeted her as she began the walk.

She'd become so proficient at packing and taking the bare minimum that her supplies never bogged her down, her shoulders never feeling the weight.

It would take her two hours alone until she reached the first game camera and another half hour after that before her first sample station, so she put her head down and spent time analyzing the data that she always had rattling around in her head.

Today was going to be a great day, she knew it. Time to put some miles under her feet.

She locked her truck and started up the trail.

The site of the first game camera always warmed her up, no matter the external temperature.

It was a personal marker for her on the hike; a quarter of the distance done.

She inspected the camera as Igor had previously instructed.

"Always look for signs of tampering," he'd said. Seeing none, she popped the SD card out, placing a blank one back in the slot and continued on. She'd never seen much on any of the collected cards before, but Igor had software that helped change the tint and brightness further on the video. One time he'd found some footage of a rare bird on a branch that she couldn't make out when she first watched it.

Continuing on, she arrived at her sample site. Here she removed her pack and pulled out her containers. She prided herself on being meticulous about her collection samples, so her various Tupperware was placed specifically in order based on the sample sites she'd visit.

Grabbing a drink from her canteen, she surveyed the site noting no disturbances and set about collecting her samples. It only took her a few minutes, having honed her process over the course of the last few years. She replaced the Tupperware, shrugged her pack back into position and carried on. Three more game cameras, three more sample sites. The day was turning out quite well.

Sites two and three were a breeze.

She'd stopped and had a light lunch between the two locations, at a place she'd christened as her 'rest rock.' It was an oval shaped rock that allowed her to sit cross-legged on and lay out her food. It always made her feel like she was ten years old again and having a picnic.

The wind was light enough to keep her comfortable but she made a mental note that she'd need to watch how the temperature dipped as night set in. She didn't want to get caught in the cold when it was something easily preventable.

It was on the approach towards the last game camera that she came to a halt.

Something had been nagging at her for some time, but she hadn't figured it out. She'd been lost in thought, unaware of the subtle changes around her.

Now it clicked.

The forest had gone silent.

No birds, no squirrels, no wind.

Total silence.

She'd experienced this only once before, two summers ago. Her and her former boyfriend, Dmitri had went on a trip to Washington State. She'd always wanted to see the Pacific Ocean but also Portland and Seattle. They'd also explored Montana, and it was while hiking there that they realized everything had gone still. Dmitri had kept walking ahead, neither of them talking, when he suddenly put up his hand and pointed.

Ahead of them, off the trail was a large Grizzly bear.

It didn't appear to notice them. They kept their bodies facing the bear and slowly backed away until they were sure it wasn't following.

That night, Dmitri had went online and was surprised to find that while 50,000 Grizzlies still populated North America, the majority were in Alaska.

"Babe, listen to this – only about 800 Grizzly are believed to still live in Montana. Wow, what are the chances we would run into one? How cool." She didn't think it was cool.

Now, Anna had the same feeling. As though an apex predator was nearby. The area did have some black bear that lived here, but she'd never had any interactions or encounters with any of them. Normally those animals would keep their distance and retreat if humans were near.

The last game camera was set off the game trail, strapped to a tree. It was three feet off the ground. Because of its location, Anna had always considered this one her favorite. Easiest to access and easiest to put a new SD card back in.

The area the camera faced was a perfect spot to capture animals as they came and went. The trail went directly across it and the spot was a wider area than the others. The forest had helped to create a natural clearing by not having any trees grow along this section, opening a thirty-foot-wide open space.

She arrived at the camera on full alert. Something was definitely off here. She popped the SD card out, put it in its rightful spot and clipped in the new one. She made sure to see the recording light blink on and turned to leave when she caught movement.

A grey *something* rapidly fled through the trees.

Her brain tried to process it. *Was that an animal? A man?*

She listened for any sound to indicate it had stopped.

Hearing nothing, she surveyed the clearing around her, and not finding anything that caught her attention decided that whatever it was, must have been scared off when she arrived. She'd stay alert the rest of the way until her camp spot, but just to feel a bit safer she retrieved her hunter's knife and squeezed it nice and tight in her palm. It didn't weigh much but the feeling of the steel in her hand calmed her.

She left the camera location behind, making her way towards her last station. She felt good leaving the area, but the forest reminded her that something wasn't right, staying quiet and still for another mile.

Anna arrived at the last stop and after retrieving her final samples for her own research, went about systematically setting up her camp. She'd stayed here enough times that she'd left a few things tucked away to help make things easier. It also reduced the weight she had to carry in and out. She retrieved the rope and tarp she had stowed behind some logs and stuffed in a waterproof carrying bag. She used it to set up her simple tent. She tied one end of the rope to a tree, the other to another tree, then laid the tarp over top. She then grabbed the stakes she'd left as well and hammered them into the ground with a flat rock she'd dubbed her 'stake pounder.' Once the walls of her makeshift tent were solid, she went about sorting her collected samples. While doing that she began to get a fire going and prepare a light dinner.

She'd done this enough that everything was routine – she turned into a camping robot. So much so, that she never noticed she was being watched.

As the sun dipped lower she put away her samples, knowing the bulk of her work ahead would be handled back at the lab, and leaned against her crudely fashioned chair from three pieces of wood, to watch as the stars began to twinkle and sparkle in the night sky.

It was this peace and serenity she lived for. She was the only person for miles around and to have that singular connection with the earth moved her in ways she'd never be able to describe to friends or family.

As the fire crackled and sparked beside her, she retrieved the tablet Igor had provided her to view the SD cards and make some notes regarding any notable data points on them.

She'd known Igor most of her life, and while he had his moments of buffoonery, he was her best friend and roommate and a part of her actually felt sad knowing soon they'd both be graduating and moving on with their lives.

It was an easy enough task for her to help him. She had time to kill and wasn't a big movie or TV show watcher. This felt more up her area of interest – data collection.

She'd fast forward through the game cam video – the green hue of the night vision always made her chuckle – and when she spotted movement or an animal, she'd click the time line and mark it. Then Igor would be able to quickly go through the videos on his own and not have to waste time. He'd give her $20 for each SD card she marked for him, so it was a fair trade in her mind.

She slipped the first SD card in – her analytical OCD dictated she watch them in order – and got comfortable as the forest on the screen came alive. She always marveled at how many animals she'd get to witness through this little device, animals she'd never come across otherwise. Unlike humans, animals never changed their behavior if they knew a camera was around. She'd seen some clips over her time doing this reconnaissance work for Igor, where animals came right up and sniffed the camera, inspecting this robotic intrusion into its environment. For the most part, the animals either ignored it or were ignorant to its spying.

She fast forwarded the current video for three hours of footage time before she caught some movement and hit pause. Returning the speed to normal she watched as a family of mice came into view and scurried about on the ground. She sped up the video again and after two more hours slowed it back down as three fox entered the frame. They nibbled some leaves and dug at the ground.

Not much going on, she thought as she marked that sighting and decided to move onto the next card. She'd return to this one later if she had time.

The second card was full of critters. The camera was set up in a spot that looked over a small water source as well as a number of bushes with berries on it. She saw squirrels and even a rabbit. This time of year most of these animals were passing through, heading to wherever they'd burrow and hunker down for the winter.

The fire popped and spit out a large spark, causing her to jump. She hadn't realized she was so on edge. She poked at the coals with the stick she'd fashioned just for the job, then tossed another piece of wood on, getting the flames roaring again. It was once the fire calmed after the initial fuel that something caught her attention.

She lowered the tablet, letting her eyes adjust back to the limited lighting around the campsite. The tablet was set to a low level, but it was still significantly brighter than what the wilderness provided.

She could hear a rhythmic sound from far off in the woods. A *dum... dum... dum... dum...* It was as though drums were echoing through the mountains.

It made her skin crawl and the hair on her head pull tight to her scalp. She'd always loved the quiet aloneness of this place. Tonight, she wished she was anywhere else in the world.

"*Hoooooooooooeeeeeeeeeee.*"

The howl cut through the darkness. She grabbed her knife from where she kept it on the ground by her leg and retrieved another stick she kept by the fire. This one was wrapped with some bark at the end. Dipping it into the fire, she held it there while it caught, all the while she was scanning the periphery of the campsite.

She could hear something moving in her direction, crashing through the trees. She held the torch out in front of her, the other hand extended with the knife thrust out.

The sound continued approaching. Whatever was causing it would be coming out into view shortly. She prepared herself, ready for some sort of confrontation.

Four roe deer burst forth from the darkness of the woods, coming to a halt when they spotted her standing with the burning branch and knife. They turned and fled back into the trees, back to making their racket as they disappeared.

"Jesus Christ," she said, as she exhaled. She sat down, let her breathing calm. She was surprised with how amped up she'd become, but it made sense after the oddness of the forest on her hike.

Flipping the tablet back on, she didn't see the figures sit down at the edge of the trees, legs crossed beneath them. If Anna hadn't been so frightened she would have clued in that the deer were running *from* something, not just making their way through the woods.

The rest of this particular card was boring. Some small rodents and birds. She marked the spots and popped out the SD card. She looked at the time, not realizing it was already near ten. She decided to go through the last card she'd collected and get some sleep. She'd found in her experience that the last game camera had the most action because of its location.

She hit the play button and was immediately rewarded with a lynx padding by. She'd never seen one previously on any of the cards, so she marked it and made a mental note to remember to share the good news with Igor when she got home. She resumed the fast forward, watching as nothing happened. The trees moved and swayed from the subtle wind, which was only noticeable during the faster speed.

She was a bit surprised to see no animals during the rest of the first day of recording as she went through. She was about four hours into the first night on the recording, when she caught movement in the trees. She backed it up and returned the playback speed to normal. She watched, keenly trying to spot it again.

There it was.

She felt her blood run cold as she watched a grey shape move through the trees. It was set back just enough into the woods that the camera couldn't pick up a completely defined animal. She realized this might be the same thing she'd spotted earlier. Same shape, color and size.

She went back again, slowing the playback down even more and brought the tablet closer to her face, squinting to try and make out what it was she was seeing.

Unfortunately the green tinge of the night vision made it impossible for her to get any sharp edges. The shape remained a blurry *thing*.

She sped up the video a bit, watching as this blur moved back and forth, seemingly having no purposeful reason for the pattern. Then a deer entered closer to the camera, causing the video to focus on it. The deer walked tentatively, ears up. It was on alert and as it nosed around through the grass, Anna watched as its head snapped to attention. Then the blur from the trees was moving, the deer turned and sprinted away and the blur left the camera shot, disappearing after the animal.

"What the hell?" Anna said out loud, the fire popping as if to attempt a reply.

She sped up the video, looking for any more signs of the shape, but nothing came about. A few minutes later, the video showed the sun rise and the darkness give way to daylight.

Anna felt her pulse quicken again as she picked up movement on the screen, only to breathe out a sigh of relief when she saw it was just a bird flying into the shot. She sped up the playback again, noticing all was still. Not even the trees were moving in the back. The wind had died down, which was odd for the location.

She paused here, poking the fire, getting the flames to rise up again. She'd felt the cold starting to set in, but she wasn't ready to call it a night.

Not now.

She started the video, pausing when the next night arrived. The game cam was unique in that it would always soft record, but would delete video that didn't feature anything dubbed 'extra activity' each day. This allowed for large sections of time to not need to be sped through. In fact, entire days wouldn't exist, if no animals didn't happen by.

Night arrived on the camera and she found she had tensed, expecting something to pop up on the screen again. Her breath was fogging up the screen, she'd pulled it so close. She took a second, focused on relaxing and letting her breathing settle.

Once she felt in control, she pressed play and sped up the video.

At first there was nothing. Just trees and green hue.

Soon she spotted something glowing, the night vision causing whatever it was that was emitting the light to flare and distort the picture. She waited for the camera to adjust and focus, and when it did she let out a gasp.

She watched as five figures walked along the edge of the trees holding torches. They paused when they were in the middle of the screen, turned towards the game camera, then turned again and carried on their way. It was as though they'd paraded by and stopped, specifically to let whoever was recording see them.

Her brain started to race. She was trying to simultaneously process what she'd seen but also talk herself out of the truth, that what she'd spotted earlier, the movement, was the same thing she was now looking at.

Someone had been watching her earlier.

Out here, in the middle of nowhere, others were in the forest.

And they'd been near her.

This realization caused her world to slowly start to distort. She felt isolated, small; betrayed by the forest. The trees all looked at her menacingly, as though they'd been conspiring against her since the beginning. She'd never once felt unsafe coming out here by herself. She trusted her survival instincts and her strength. But now she wasn't so sure. There had been five figures on that video.

Her senses flared as though suffering a seizure. She could feel the soil through her shorts, could hear the smallest movements within the trees.

Anna halted, focused. Letting everything settle. She knew she'd need to watch more of the video, see if there was more on it, but the thought of doing that scared her to her core.

She counted to three and hit play again. The video jumped to life. It was still night, but the figures had disappeared. She sped up the playback, anticipating what was to come. She checked the time stamp, seeing that it was now speeding through two in the morning, then three. At four, she saw something on the edge of the screen and stopped the fast forward. She reversed it and waited for whatever it was to return.

On the far left of the screen she saw something shift. A set of curved horns appeared on the periphery of the video. They bucked and jumped, but whatever it was they were attached onto didn't show itself.

That's odd, she thought. *Those look like mountain sheep horns.* But this area wasn't home to a population of those mammals.

She knew she should be getting her ass out of there. Nothing had felt right since arriving at the game camera and spotting that movement. Things had been *off* and she should have been smarter. Now, even though she knew the trail like it was her apartment, it was simply too dark for her to make her way back out at night.

The scene transfixed her as she watched the horns buck and thrash. Then she watched as a figure, a *creature* was pulled by a chain into view. This *person*, if that was the correct word, was nude from the neck down. A thick shackle was around its neck, a robed figure was yanking and pulling on the chain that was attached to the collar. The chained person didn't have a human head. This was something Anna was struggling with, fighting with. They appeared to have the head of a goat. Two thickened, curled horns protruded and came around beside their snout. They fought and kicked, before another robbed figure appeared and pressed a flaming torch into the midsection of this figure. Although there was no sound, Anna could almost hear the tortured braying coming from its open mouth.

She watched as the figure dragged the creature into the trees at the back of the screen. She didn't look away until the blurred light of the torches disappeared.

Once they were gone she closed the tablet, finding she was now shaking uncontrollably.

Just what the fuck was going on?

She heard a shuffling noise from her left, but when she looked saw nothing. Everything felt uneven now, as though the ground of the forest had developed mold and the spores were bubbling and shifting beneath her feet.

She went to stand when she felt a presence to her right. She swung as hard as she could, knowing it was a life or death. Whatever was there grabbed her arm and twisted before she was forced to the ground. She felt a cloth cover her mouth and breathed in an odd aroma. Everything went dizzy as a thick sack was placed over her head.

Anna came back with the sack still over her head.

She was on her knees, arms bound behind her back. While the sack was a tightly weaved material she could still catch the flicker of flames between some of the fibers.

All around her she could hear hand clapping, foot stomping and a rhythmic swishing.

The sack created a claustrophobic pressure on her face. She tried twisting and turning, wanting to open up some room so she could at least breathe, but the more she struggled the tighter it felt.

As she started gasping for air, the sack was ripped off her head and the sight before her made her wish it hadn't.

Three flat rocks.

On each one, a naked, goat-headed figure lay bound.

It was impossible to completely comprehend the abominations that struggled and strained against their bindings.

She was hauled to her feet and dragged forward between two of the rocks until they were at the head of the middle rock. Looking around, she saw that a semi-circle of robbed figures surrounded them. They continued clapping their hands and stomping their feet.

As the clapping and stomping reached a crescendo, she wished she could cover her ears, do something to stop the vibrations the sound was causing in her head.

Then it abruptly stopped.

A figure stepped forward from the crowd, its robe black instead of grey like the others.

It removed the hood, exposing its own set of gnarled horns.

"Hoooooooooooeeeeeeeeeee," they screamed, which prompted the rest of the figures to pull back their hoods.

Anna found herself surrounded by two dozen horned men. They all possessed human bodies with animal heads. Not one single set of horns was the same; all curved and curled differently. The ridges and edges as unique as a fingerprint.

She wanted to scream and run. *How was this even possible?*

Instead, she felt her legs turn to mush, her body falling to the ground. The figures supporting her jabbed her and forced her back to a standing position.

She was pulled forward, beside the middle figure. Her arms placed over the head of the restrained individual.

A second figure joined her, holding a bowl. They placed some leaves and twigs into the bowl and set it on the rock. Producing a knife, they sliced their left forearm. Letting some of the blood drip into the bowl, it started grinding and mashing, producing a thick greenish-red paste.

Once it was done, the figure spread some of the paste on Liz's forearm, which immediately burned.

She squirmed and grimaced as it grew hotter, but soon felt a cooling relief. Opening her eyes she saw the creature from the rock licking her arm, sloppily ingesting the paste.

She felt her stomach churn at the sensation of its meaty tongue rolling across her skin.

Before she could puke, she was pushed to the far left rock, where the paste was reapplied and the creature molested her forearm with its tongue. It was then repeated with the creature on the far right rock. By the time all three had licked up the mush from her skin, it was blistered and seared.

Tears streamed down her face as she was forced back onto her knees.

This is it, she thought. *This is when I die.*

The clapping and stomping started again and the creature that had made the paste walked up to her, knelt down so that it was face to face. Anna saw that it was holding another sack in its hands.

"For Father."

"For Father!" the rest chanted over and over.

"Now you know," someone whispered into her ear, before they covered her face once again with a cloth and she tumbled into an unconscious state.

It was the chirping of a bird and the feeling of gravel that brought her from her stupor.

She rolled over, finding herself still clad in the sack.

Scrambling, she was able to easily pull it off and was shocked to discover her location.

She was back at her truck.

Getting to her feet, she used her vehicle to get her legs under her, finding the effects of whatever knocked her out fading away. Where the paste had been was inflamed and red, but something had been coated on her skin. She took in the parking area, searching for any signs of the figures she'd encountered. Confident that she was alone and free to leave, she grabbed her backpack and supplies that had been neatly stacked by the front tire.

She could feel eyes on her. Just because she couldn't see *them*, didn't mean they weren't watching. This was the lesson she'd learned. The forest and its creatures were always watching.

She gathered her belongings and put them on the passenger seat of the truck.

She climbed in behind the wheel and felt some anxiety wash away when the vehicle started just fine.

Anna backed the truck up slowly, expecting an ambush.

With the truck now facing the road, she shifted into drive and hit the gas, accelerating faster than normal. She didn't care. She needed to put some miles between her and her former research site.

There was no chance she'd ever return.

If she was being honest, she doubted she could ever enter any woods, ever again, no matter where they were. What this meant for her future and her career aspirations, she wasn't sure. She'd cross that bridge once necessary.

As the truck bounced along the road, she heard a rattling coming from the passenger side floor. She hadn't noticed the sack that had been placed there.

Once she spotted it, she slammed on the brakes.

Anna picked up the sack and dumped the contents onto the seat.

Seeing the pair of horns tumbling out, she knew she'd been marked.

Her forearm burned as she started driving again, knowing that no matter where she went, the creatures would always be with her.

Always watching.

Now you know.

For Father.

END

BOOK OF LIES

The Book of Lies was a tome discovered in the wilderness in Russia.

Near a circle of ruins, not far from an abandoned building, it was said to be found under the remains of hundreds of corpses – both human and animals.

Eleven sections made of eleven sentences that relate to the eleven cosmic chaos gods, The Book of Lies is not an easy read and when read aloud following certain ceremonies can and will conjure forth unwanted entities from other realms.

Long kept under lock and key, The Book of Lies has recently been revealed to hold the true directions to unlock and open the door.

The door that leads to the Black Heavens.

1 before there was light, before there was dark, there was only chaos

2 energy, unharnessed awaiting a destination

3 for the blackness would swirl and the stars would anguish

4 until the chaos consumed, bred

5 converted its purpose

6 and from that hatred, a species arrived

7 the earth was born from the eleven spectral deities

8 chaos leading the way

9 the masses converged and separated, pushed and pulled by the torment of the debacherous power that had arrived

10 before, from the shadows, stepping forth into the light, the chosen one stood high

11 taking its place as the opener of the black heavens, the savior, coming from hoof and horn high above on stone

BOOK TWO

SUMMONS

1 called forth from the depths of blackness; "ARISE" they shall call to summons

2 cast away rejoice, come, COME JOIN the anointed and be one with the flock

3 for a group shall coexist, live harmoniously as family, blood within blood, love shared and burgeoning serenity

4 the steps taken with care; foot after foot, one before the other, balance begets persistence

5 "ARISE" it shall shout, from high up near the heavens to the bottom of the well; "ARISE" as we summon

6 and from the well they will cheer and rejoice as the savior is amongst them, there to lead those who've strayed back to salvation

343

7 eternal life is a truth, the singular truth to let into the soul

8 amongst the black heavens, amongst the cosmic chaos with dust and ruin and flesh

9 from hoof and horn the flock will be summoned, gathered to dance and rejoice

10 the knowledge shared shall be the blood life of all

11 summon and revel in the cosmic immortality of forever

1 "My CHILDREN of CHAOS. I speak to you, for you, from within you, you're one and only Lord and Savior.

2 the conflagration will engulf those unworthy, so bow and accept my word as Law.

3 as your leader and teacher, I am divine.

4 tether your holy worth to my seed and together and only then shall we ascend into immortality.

5 from hoof and horn I have been deemed righteous and of true spirit

6 to accept MY word is to accept chaos divinity

7 bow; BOW before me and scrape thy knee and thy breast on the floor of sins

8 it flows, YES, it flows through us; a pulse from the horned one himself

9 while its heart beats and I possess it, the portal shall remain open and pure

10 pledge thy service and thy soul to ME and only ME

11 as fealty shall ensure acceptance as the blackness swirls and grasps."

BOOK FOUR
GRATITUDE

1 worthfulness shall be shown through fealty agreed upon

2 a joyous member is one to accept, engulf allow entry into the hearts of those around them

3 those bowed have exposed their true nature and their soul is connected to hoof and horn through significant love

4 for someone to show without worry of harm nor scorn is truly pure of heart and soul

5 blackness illuminated to light

6 a circle will be drawn and those who have stepped within have the gratitude of the cosmos

7 eleven thanks, eleven points for the soul to ascend

8 a shining star alone in the darkened sky beams upon the smiling heart

9 for the end is the beginning, a circular journey of immortal lust

10 a man, a woman, a hoof, a horn

11 OUR gratitude to those who aid in opening the black heavens

BOOK FIVE
CHAOS

1 oh, how glorious the black heavens will be!

2 infinite light, infinite dark, holy hands held as your soul connects

3 all will dance and sway and share the joy of never ending life!

4 a cosmic swirling of decay, made all the more whole by the drowning of the ground

5 celestial bodies connect and fuse, transforming into a sacred pilgrimage

6 "but what will we see?" the curious will ask. "What awaits our immortal soul?"

7 severed from the gravity of earth, the chosen shall fly free from the surface and be holy in the scattered luminescence

349

8 a strong sense of faith and belief in hoof will let you be selected to stand shoulder to shoulder with the dark ones

9 imagine a future of no time, no day, no night, just orgiastic providence

10 belief will flounder within the slaughtered, but have determination of sacrifice for purpose

11 for only sacrifice will let your cosmic parts arrive and be accepted within the black heavens

BOOK SIX
ENSLAVEMENT

1 corrupted by visions of faith, the flock must accept their roles and positions

2 enslavement allows the soul to be penetrated.

3 one by one, on and on the masses must kneel and become willing participants

4 masks and horns, knowledge and chaos

5 insolence will not be tolerated, the one in power will lash out and demand servitude

6 stripped of cloth, hair and title, the weak shall be built up while the strong will be beaten into submission

7 "You will be part of the journey," hoof and horn will promise, as long as an understanding has been accepted

351

8 "Join us in our mission, of everlasting blackness and decay."

9 for the pathway has been long followed, the way forward much the same as the way back

10 ignorance will be an unworthy excuse for insubordination

11 "Arise as faithful, one by one for chaos has decided to accept all of its slaves into the black heavens"

1 within its grasp; a sacrifice follows a sacrifice

2 of hoof and horn shall choose the everlasting soul to harness chaos and live amongst man

3 they will usher in the masses, retrieve and convey the black heavens importance

4 a figure of stature and status; a Father to lead and succeed; He of great devotion and unfailing desire

5 "GATHER MY CHILDREN, REPENT THY SINS," for forgiveness is acceptance and the gates will only open to those willing to reveal their true nature

6 man helpeth man, woman helpeth woman, children will be subjected to scrutiny and standards of cleanliness

7 to step forward from the shadow, to transcend the blackest matter into light and lead the parish into chaos, only the strong can contend with inexorable acceptance

8 "for I am whole and the gates have opened" shall be whispered into their ear

9 blood will flow as the knife slits the soul, blood will pool and dampen desire

10 but for those who see the rise and the nature of future blessings, will ultimately follow

11 for on the day of enlightenment, the day of self-sacrifice, only then will immortality befriend death

BOOK EIGHT
RITUAL

1 for the one will be chosen, named such of nature to be true

2 all must be in place and practiced, everything just so

3 he of normality and routine, a human respective of knowledge and repetition

4 like a goat in sheep's clothing they will be spotted within the masses

5 a pupil of our Lord, a devourer of scripture

6 "Memorize the tasks. Mundane as they appear."

7 they will play a part in connectivity, chaos and breeding

8 "Look for a sign. A notice. A reason. A false throne will be provided for the Ritual to occur."

9 "Sheol, bringing of death. Abbadon our Lord and Saviour. Arise and fornicate with your concubines, with your outlets to cross the void."

10 for an awakening has begun, the black heavens hear the cries.

11 of hoof and horn will sever the heads and move on.

BOOK NINE
COMMUNION

1 consume that which has been offered, my friends!

2 to dine with the neighbor is to share and shed blood with true friends

3 travel through and across the celestial acreage

4 for an innocent shall inherit the source and when they look upon the Mother of the flame, they'll know that the hole in thy head was purposeful

5 divinity awaits, shared from true menstrual prophecy

6 awakened by hoof and horn, awakened by the language of the ancient prophets

7 receptive in nature makes a chosen soul worth walking the darkness beside

8 dance! Dance with our love and dance with each other for the holiest of ascension will be upon you shortly

9 grab our hands and let the darkness drain down our throats

10 as the gates open and call us into its heavenly bosom we'll be content knowing we've left our earthly horrors behind

11 come, come with us as we celebrate forever amongst the cosmos together!

BOOK TEN
SACRAMENT

1 a book is but words to guide the wayward soul

2 man must emulate the true vision of our Lord, of hoof and horn

3 to be guided from soil to stars, to be accepted from solid to chaos

4 our eternal spirit and immortal happiness will unlock an everlasting pilgrimage

5 read what is written, ingest what is offered, absorb what is slathered

6 fluids shared will highlight the decency required for allowance

7 when the dust is settled and the scorned have been eradicated

8 man, woman and child shall stand shoulder to shoulder with hoof and horn

9 the great mass will begin, the throngs walking as one, hoofed and horned

10 for our savior has spoken the gospel and the gates have opened and await

11 the black heavens greet all with chaos and pain

BOOK ELEVEN
RESURRECTION

1 find solace through looking for the one true seal

2 for the congregation shall come together

3 a world of ash and depravity await even the hardiest of believers

4 "come one, come all and listen to the great deceiver!"

5 returned to the corporeal will subject the man to nature

6 remember the laws of animal and the heavens

7 arise again from the soot and the sulphur

8 a beast of hoof and horn shall allow you place to worship

9 for the red will shine down on thee and those anointed

10 worthy of eternal sacrifice and servitude

11 in the forgotten eyes of the one true leader, arise and follow the beast.

By Mason McDonald

I've designed plenty of covers for Steve. From his wonderful The Boy Whose Room Was Outside to the twisted Wagon Buddy series to — my personal favorite of his work — Yuri, but none have been as fun and satisfying as his Father of Lies trilogy. They are stories that showcase raw, depraved, bleak, no-light-at-the-end-of-this-fucking-tunnel horror on full display. This universe is a bus with a bomb in the back and some snipped break lines plowing full-tilt into a gaggle of Nuns. It is violent, horrific, unflinching, and I was honored he chose me to design the covers.

Steve and I have been friends for a few years now, meeting on Twitter, and I can honestly call him the best friend I've never met. We met in 2018 when we exchanged stories like mixtapes and quickly became pals. I had published a few short stories myself by that point and had designed my own covers. By that point I believe Steve only had one or two published works — unbelievable, right? The guy's published approximately five books just in the time it took me to write this — and he asked me for help with designing something for his next release. I said no problem, of course.

I had no idea that agreeing to help with one cover would prosper into one of the best relationships I have in this industry, if not the best.

Since then I have designed so many covers for him I couldn't begin to name them all. When I try, I forget certain designs or I leave out important elements, or I just plain old mix up covers I designed and others that I didn't. What I don't forget, however, and what I could never forget, is his story Ritual.

Steve and I had been working on separate submissions for an open call for an anthology I can no longer remember. We exchanged said stories on the basis we would beta read for one another. The story I sent him was a forgettable gothic tale that I have tried to erase from my mind (for good reason, trust me) and the one he sent me was what would become Ritual.

How can I describe what reading Ritual for the first time was like, even in its primitive, shorter version?

How does one describe being utterly disgusted, terrified, and repulsed while at the same time being totally enveloped in story and character and fantastic prose? It's quite easy, actually. You say that you just read Ritual by Steve Stred and everybody in the know will nod their heads in agreement whilst dialing up their therapist.

After both of us couldn't find homes for our stories, Steve developed his concept further and turned it into a novella. He asked if I could make the cover.

I don't think I could ever properly describe how eager I was to say yes.

Ritual is an excellent paranormal cult story that deals with demons, both internal and external. As someone born in the late 90s, my horror upbringing consisted mostly of the lull of the oos. Those of you who were there know exactly what I mean. The horror aisle of the local video store (remember those?) consisted of either classic flicks from the 80's and 90's, horrible theatrical releases like The Boogeyman (although I kind of love it) and The Grudge remake (which I sort of love even more) or the wonderfully bad straight-to-DVD films that held the majority of shelf space. Those movies are my childhood. I wouldn't be who I am today without those horribly wondrous post-90's gems so believe me when I make this next comparison, it is not one I make easily or without serious contemplation.

Ritual reads like the best of them and gives off every vibe they did, only stronger, thicker, more robust and complete. When I finished it I put it down and just sat there, over-whelmed by the nostalgic tidal wave that washed over me. Maybe I am alone in this comparison. Probably I am. But I don't care. Ritual, in my opinion, would have been right at home up on the shelf in the corner, away from where all the decent folk would see them, next to all my favorite movies.

So when I was tasked with designing a cover, I knew exactly what well to draw my inspiration from. I'm not sure if I succeeded in capturing that feeling, but I think I did. I hope I did.

Steve must have liked it because he asked me to do the sequel, and the sequel's sequel, and then the book you're reading now. The rest, as they say, is history.

These stories are mean. They are unforgiving. They will

make you turn away, they will make you look for the pause button, they will make you want to eject the disc and throw it at the pimply-faced little fucker behind the counter at Blockbuster and demand your money back for allowing you to leave their place of business with such filth.

Just like all my favorite movies did.

And yours too, I imagine.

So read these stories. Love them like I do. If you like the covers, thank you. If you don't, I don't really care. Because on Christmas morning, no one gives a shit about the wrapping paper. The goodies inside are what we all want. And trust me, you want these stories.

Before I let you go, I offer some advice. Take it from someone who knows; if Steve Stred ever invites you to Sunday Mass, please, just decline politely. He's a good guy. A great one, actually.

But you don't want to meet what he worships.

Mason McDonald
    April 30th, 2021

THE BATTLE RAGED ON AND ON
ANSWERING READER'S QUESTIONS

So, by this point you've read how I joined a cult and wrote these three novellas (and a bonus fourth story). You may ask, what else can I add to this?

A few things, I think. Or more specifically I can answer some questions that have come up.

For one, people have asked about whether I actually did join a cult.

The answer to that is complicated, but for the simple answer – yes.

You see, I was researching a specific cult sect/offshoot and in order to get deeper or really, to cultivate more material, I had to play the game and do as asked. There were certainly things I wouldn't do, but I was able to do just enough to see into the inner workings. Now, they may have been talking shit about me and my unwillingness to do other aspects, but I'll never know.

Why didn't I screenshot stuff?

Very common thought here. I'm not very techie, so I can't speak on that side of it. All I know is that using the Tor browser and being let into the message board and the group chat, I was unable to take a real, non-blurry screenshot. I tried. Oh, I tried. But sadly, whatever was in place to block access also had some odd scrambling effect.

Do I believe in demons?

I had a reader message me on Goodreads about this. I don't know. Honestly. The photos and video I saw still creep me out to this day, but as someone who doesn't completely believe in a Heaven or Hell, I have to wrap my head around the biblical implications of a 'demon' as those do have some Christian undertones. I know other cultures do have demons, but the Heaven and Hell aspect really moves it towards that area.

So, while I may not believe completely in 'demons' per say, I do believe there are things unseen, things best left alone out there in the cosmos. It could also have been photo shopped for shock effect. Hard to say.

Do I still visit the cult online?

No. I actually haven't been on since 'Sacrament' came out. I think a big part of that was deleting the Tor browser as well as being so focused on other projects. At this point, I can't see myself returning to the group or investigating them at all, but I suspect they may always be watching.

Why did you name the main guy, Brad in 'Ritual'? Pretty boring name.

I've been asked this a few times and even seen some folks grumble about it on some reviews.

The reality of it is, 99% of people who are knee deep in fanaticism or overzealous and super religious or in cults don't have crazy, insane names. Who is the most famous Scientologist? Tom Cruise? Second? John Travolta maybe? Tom and John. Not Habertik and Piutesla. I just made those up. I wanted to ground 'Ritual' in the mundane, normality of this boring guy named Brad who goes to work day in and day out. But outside of work, he reads his scripture over and over, sometimes even eating it. I included Bible quotes in the first two books to kind of mislead from The Book of Lies that Father has access to, but also to have the ambiguity of those passages be able to be used within the cult context.

Will there be more in this world?

No. I don't believe so. Not at this moment or in the immediate future. I wrote the additional fourth story 'Eucharist' to really scratch that itch for readers, but as of right now, the gates are closed and the Black Heavens are inaccessible.

Made in the USA
Coppell, TX
25 June 2022